Florence Warden

A Prince of Darkness

Vol. 2

Florence Warden

A Prince of Darkness
Vol. 2

ISBN/EAN: 9783337048075

Printed in Europe, USA, Canada, Australia, Japan

Cover: Foto ©Andreas Hilbeck / pixelio.de

More available books at **www.hansebooks.com**

A PRINCE OF DARKNESS.

A Novel.

BY

FLORENCE WARDEN,

AUTHOR OF
'THE HOUSE ON THE MARSH,' 'A DOG WITH A BAD NAME,'
'THE VAGRANT WIFE,' ETC.

IN THREE VOLUMES.
VOL. II.

LONDON:
WARD AND DOWNEY,
12, YORK STREET, COVENT GARDEN.
1885.

A PRINCE OF DARKNESS.

CHAPTER I.

THE midnight drive from Calais to " Les Bouleaux " began to seem never-ending to the occupants of the *carriole ;* they were all absorbed in such gloomy thoughts that there was a general sense of relief when Mr. Beresford lifted up his voice rather testily to complain that Gerald had scarcely spoken to him, and had told him none of the domestic news.

" Don't be disgusted, Mr. Shaw, if I seem more deeply interested in the health of the pigs and the laying of the hens than in the political crisis. In a town I am a very staunch Republican, I assure you. But in the country it is so much less important that one should have a Government than that one should have new-laid eggs. In the country alone, thank Heaven! one can ask for news and hear that there is none."

"Oh, but there is, this time, Mr. Beresford; I—I had forgotten," stammered Gerald. "Your daughter—Miss Beresford—has come; she came yesterday."

"My daughter!" cried Mr. Beresford, in astonishment, while Miss M'Leod uttered a little cry expressive of annoyance rather than any other feeling. "Why did you not tell me before?"

"I—I had forgotten," said Gerald again.

This was not quite true, but he could scarcely explain that he had found a difficulty he could not account for in introducing the young lady's name.

"She can't have produced a very strong impression, I am afraid. What is she like? I have not seen her since she was in short frocks. Come, be candid; for I don't wish to be disappointed."

"Oh, you will not be. Miss Beresford is very beautiful," said Gerald, not with enthu-

siasm, but in the manner of a cold and con-
scientious reporter.

"Ah!" said Mr. Beresford, as if relieved.
"Have the Fourniers seen her yet?"

"I think not, sir. She came yesterday
evening, and I drove back to Calais to tell
Madame Fournier of her arrival, and I spent
the night at their house. But as madame
could not come out of town to-day, and the
telegram had reached us with the news
that you would return to-night, she said
she would wait for you to introduce your
daughter."

"Yes, yes, I see. Is the girl lively and
entertaining? But I suppose you saw
scarcely anything of her."

"And were too shy to notice anything
about her? I know you, Gerald," put in
Mr. Shaw. "Are you still as much of a
woman-hater as when my tomboy daughter
Adela used to lock you into the summer-house
for saying you would never marry?"

"I don't hate women at all, Mr. Shaw,
but I don't see many at 'Les Bouleaux,' and
I don't wish to see any more."

" May you always be in as healthy a state
of mind, my boy !" said Mr. Shaw.

Mr. Beresford laughed, if the short dried-
up chuckle he uttered when his cynicism was
tickled could be called a laugh. Miss
M'Leod was heard in the darkness to rustle
with indignation at the offensive pleasantry.
Gerald's face tingled through the feeling that
he had not succeeded in being quite honest in
his last speech. He knew that he had given
the impression that he hated Miss Beresford,
or at least that he didn't want to see any
more of her ; whereas he really liked her very
much, and had been thinking all day how
much jollier " Les Bouleaux " would be now,
until she threw herself away on that
bumptious flighty Victor, who was a good
fellow enough in his way, but not half good
enough for such a dear, nice, jolly girl as she
was. So he held his tongue until they passed
through the open white gate into the long poplar
avenue, and the thud of the horse's hoofs fell
softly on the sandy road, and the tall bare trees
cracked and swung over their heads in the wind.

" Here we are !" said he then to Mr.

Shaw, who looked out before him, but was at first not particularly impressed, as not one glimmer of light from the house shone through the poplar branches to relieve the blank blackness.

It was not until they had reached the end of the avenue and gone through the second white gate into the paved courtyard that the house appeared dark and square on their right hand, and the unostentatious door which did not look in the least like a front door was thrown open, and two or three rustic figures clattered out in wooden shoes and noisily greeted the returning master. The oil-lamp which threw its feeble light on to the *carriole* through the small semicircular window over the hall-door showed the rosy and robust Delphine, who found her existence of scouring and scrubbing so delightful that she passed it in song like an operatic heroine, with intervals like the present of broadly smiling recitative. She was in her usual costume of short blue gown, loose jacket tied in round her waist with the string of her apron, and white frilled cap tied under the

chin. Marie the cook, a handsome Fleming
of two or three and thirty, whose superior
position entitled her to wear a print gown
of the lilac tint and baggy make favoured
by the British housemaid of ten years ago,
smiled a hearty welcome at her side. An
old red-eyed retriever, with a ragged coat
in colour like a door-mat of bygone times,
slunk up from the stable-yard to sniff round
the heels of his master as he descended from
the *carriole*, and to leap up on his shoulders
and lick his face with demonstrative fondness
as Mr. Beresford drew his paralysed leg slowly
to the ground. At the back of the group
stood Henri the coachman, an old retainer
whose only fault was that he had now grown
so fat that except on occasions of state and
ceremony his weight and the large space he
filled in the carriage obliged him to be left at
home : his round light eyes, which looked
like pale marbles, were fixed on his master's
stooping figure with steadiness which meant,
what they could not express, that he was
glad to see him back again. The dog barked
and the rustic retinue loudly murmured such a

chorus of unaffected welcome that Mr. Shaw's
spirits recovered from their depression as
Delphine, who was as muscular as she was
merry, caught sight of him, cried out enthusi-
astically, "Encore un monsieur!" and almost
lifted him to the ground. Then she gave a
hearty slap on the back to Gerald, and, in a
confidential whisper, which Mr. Shaw half
heard and wholly misinterpreted, told the
young gentleman that the day had been long
without him to somebody. And on Mr.
Shaw's ears, as he followed his host into the
house, fell words of haughty animosity in
scarcely intelligible patois, between the two
deadly enemies, whose ambushes with pails of
water and attacks with blacking-brushes kept
the quiet household in perpetual ferment when
Mr. Beresford was at " Les Bouleaux :" these
were the two men-servants, fat Henri and thin
Pierre, whose rivalry in their master's esteem
was a fierce torrent which nothing could stem.

As the gentlemen entered the tiled hall,
which was quite bare with the exception
of a strip of matting from end to end, an
umbrella-stand, and some hat-pegs, a door

immediately facing the front door opened, and
a pale little lady in a black stuff gown, looking
as insignificant as only pale little women in
mourning can look, appeared at the opening.
The expression of her face was both sullen and
woe-begone, and she stared straight at Mr.
Beresford with black eyes which almost
said : " This is even worse than I expected."

If she was disappointed in her father, he
was still more disappointed in his daughter ;
he walked past her into the first *salon,*
sat down in the straight-backed carved arm-
chair by the stove, and after telling Marie to
show Mr. Shaw to the spare room, said,
without turning to his daughter, " Come
here."

She crossed the polished floor obediently,
and stood before him like a child who has
been scolded and who doesn't mean to be
good.

" What is your name ?"

" My name !"

" Yes.   Your Christian name, of course.
I have forgotten it."

" Peggy ; at least—Margaret."

" Peggy-at-least-Margaret !"

" I believe it was by your wish that I was christened Margaret, so mamma always called me Peggy."

" Then in future you will be Margaret—you understand ?"

" Yes."

The tone was sullenly docile, but if he had looked up at that moment he would have seen on the little white face, with its delicately aquiline features and tiny curled mouth, an expression of elfin malignity which would have entirely justified his philosophical lack of paternal tenderness.

" You know why I sent for you ?"

" Yes ; to marry me to some one."

" Yes." A pause. "I thought you would be more—more like your mother. She was a very handsome woman."

" She was always complaining that I was more—more like you."

The gray head was slowly raised, and the girl trembled a little with sudden recognition of her own boldness as her black eyes met the

steady gaze of the grave old man. He did
not look angry and he did not look amused;
but her audacity evidently gave her some
sort of standing in his eyes, and his tone
when he next addressed her was less curt,
though no warmer than before.

"I am afraid you have suffered from the
unfortunate incompatibility of your parent's
temper, Margaret. And perhaps it was your
unlucky likeness to your father which pre-
vented your mother from doing her best for
you."

"She couldn't make me beautiful, if that
is what you mean."

"But she might have taught you to dress
better, and to hold yourself better. I don't
mean to be unkind, but your appearance
suggests rather a post-office clerk, or a paid
companion, than—than Miss Beresford."

"Well, that is what Miss Beresford would
have had to be, if you had not sent for her
to fill a position for which she is far less
suited."

"I don't know about 'far less suited.'
You can make answers which are smart, even

if they are rather rude. And I suppose you could dress well and look well if you had money, and knew where to spend it. You look rather handsome, too, now that you are indignant, and marriage would give you plenty of opportunities for that. How did your mother spend her allowance? On dress for herself, I suppose?"

" Yes, partly. The allowance wasn't handsome enough for us both to dress well, while, for the sake of what shifting position we had, it was better that one at least shouldn't look quite like a rag-picker."

" You are rather daring in your similes, for a lady."

" A lady who has to wander about the world as I have done becomes daring in more things than similes."

She looked like a little Amazon by this time, and no bearing could have been more erect than hers as she drew herself up, and gradually raised a rather graceful little head to an angle expressive of open defiance.

" Now, if you would always carry your head like that you would be all right," said her father persuasively, quite ignoring the defiance. "Do try, there's a good child, and open that door and see if there is anything to eat on the table."

She obeyed rather awkwardly, feeling that the boiling excitement to which she had raised herself during their short conversation should have been used for better things than a mere summons to supper. As she opened the door of the *salle-à-manger*, Miss M'Leod, too evidently retreating from the keyhole, met her and looked at her with a disagreeable expression of mingled jealousy and contempt. A dear good little woman she was, this pocket-sized housekeeper, with principles so very high that now and then they could not be brought down to the vulgar level of daily life, and so they got lost sight of for a time.

"Is Mr. Beresford ready for supper?" she asked, with the double-distilled haughtiness of a great personage caught in an evil deed.

Without waiting for an answer, she swept past the young girl, and re-entered the *salle-à-manger* with the crippled gentleman leaning on her arm, just as the door from the hall opened, and Mr. Shaw and Gerald came in, both laughing.

" Pierre and Henri are at it again already," said Gerald, as he took his seat at the table.

" What's the matter now ?"

" Henri has discovered a mystery, and Pierre won't believe in it. So they are exhausting their powers of invective at the bottom of the staircase. Neither of them would be alive to-morrow morning if they dared fight; but Henri daren't hit out because he can't run, and Pierre can't see where to hit at all. But the faculty of speech is only too well preserved in both of them."

" What is it all about ?"

" Oh, Henri declares that a bolt has been placed on one of the kitchen-doors within the last twenty-four hours, that it has been placed there for some nefarious purpose, and that the person who placed it there is Monnier, the head game-keeper."

Everybody laughed. The allegation was mild compared to some of the tales of poison and sorcery with which at different times Henri had sought to compass his rival's ruin.

"Monnier! not Pierre!" exclaimed Mr. Beresford, in astonishment.

"Well, you see, Pierre hasn't been in the house five minutes, while the bolt has been on the door some hours. Even Henri's brilliant imagination couldn't get over that difficulty."

"What bolt is it? And why is poor old Monnier dragged into the story?"

"Henri's tale is that this afternoon, while both the women were upstairs, he was in his own room next to the stable, when he saw Monnier cross the end of the yard, and go round towards the back door. Knowing that it was the time when there would be nobody downstairs, he went out to tell Monnier so, expecting to find him vainly knocking. But instead of that he looked through the scullery window, and saw Monnier open the door leading into the kitchen. Monnier just nodded to him, and he went back to the stable; but when he came in to fetch his tea he declares that he discovered a new and unaccountable bolt on the kitchen-door."

"What an old fool it is!" said Mr. Beresford. " I shall have to send him and Pierre about their business together."

" Oh, don't do that !" said the kind-hearted housekeeper.

" My dear lady, isn't one decrepit old man in the house enough, without a doddering retinue of chattering old mystery-mongers, who haven't his one virtue of occasional silence ?"

She bowed her head quite meekly; and Gerald went on :

" I really think, though, sir, that for the first time in his life Henri may have blundered upon something worth investigating."

Not having yet recovered from the shock of the robbery in the train, they all, with the exception of Miss Beresford, who had not heard of the affair, turned towards him with a morbid feeling of being prepared for horrors. He laughed somewhat uneasily, as he looked round at their faces, all expressing a sentiment from which he himself was not free.

" It is nothing very dreadful—at least, I hope not," he said, lowering his voice.

"But from one or two little things, which I will tell you about presently, I can't help fancying Monnier knows something about the robberies which have taken place here lately."

"My dear fellow, be careful what you say," said Mr. Beresford.

Everybody was getting excited. Miss Beresford, who was sitting by Gerald, but of whom he had throughout the meal taken no notice, looked like an elf under a mushroom, as she leaned over the table to get a clear view of the speaker's face, crouching on her elbow, with wide-open black eyes, her pouting red lips parted, and her black hair and eyebrows giving intensity to the eager expression of her white face. Mr. Shaw, who got unhappy if he was left long out of a conversation, had his mouth open, ready to drop in, on the first chance, with a monologue. Miss M'Leod tried not to look frightened, but glanced at the clock, and wished they wouldn't talk about this sort of thing so near bed-time. But Mr. Beresford insisted on hearing Gerald out.

"I wouldn't say such a thing without some proof, sir," said the latter, in a low voice. "But I know there has been a stranger about Monnier's cottage lately, for I've seen him there myself; and last night I found little Jules Benoit hiding under a bush, calling out: 'Oh, M. Monnier, I won't tell! And I didn't see anything, indeed!' Of course, these things don't prove anything; but they seem a little suspicious when there's robbery going on, don't they?"

"And do you think he committed the robbery in the train?" panted Miss M'Leod, in a whisper.

"What robbery? When?" hissed out Miss Beresford, in the same key.

But the gentlemen were too preoccupied to answer them.

"Go on, Gerald," said Mr. Beresford briefly. "When did you see the man at Monnier's? What was he like?"

"He was tall, and slim, and dark. I thought at first it was Victor come to spoon Babette."

These words had scarcely slipped out of

his mouth when he heartily repented his in-
discretion, as a sudden movement of the girl
by his side attracted his attention to her, and
he saw a swift look of anger and shame pass
over her face.

" He looked like a gentleman, then ?" said
Mr. Beresford, surprised.

" From the little I saw of him—yes."

" How many times have you seen him ?"

" Only once : last Wednesday week—the
day Dupont was robbed."

Mr. Beresford considered a moment ; then
he said : " Gerald, would you mind sending
Pierre up to my room and the rest to bed ?
Keep Marie back a minute, and ask *her* about
the bolt : her brain is not made of cotton-
wool, like the others'."

Gerald obeyed. One of the doors of the
salle-à-manger opened into a passage which
led from the hall to the servants' offices,
which were on the same modest scale as the
rest of the little country house. Having dismissed the rest of the servants, elicited from
Marie the confession that she really could not
say whether the bolt Henri had pointed out

was there before or not, and sent her after the others, Gerald went through the kitchen into the large roughly-paved scullery beyond, and, by the light of the lamp, had just discovered a tiny bolt, fixed at the very top of the door, when the sound of a man's footsteps made him start. It was Mr. Shaw, who came whispering and sliding round the door from the kitchen. Gerald pointed to the bolt, and said nobody remembered whether it had been there before to-day or not; while the elder man fetched a wooden chair, and by the help of the lamp examined the bolt thoroughly.

"It is an old bolt," said he, "but it has been recently put on."

"Well, what does it mean?" asked Gerald, struck by the solemnity of the tone of his old friend.

"It means that there is something wrong with your old friend Monnier, my boy, and it looks as if he intended using Mr. Beresford's scullery either as a refuge or a rendezvous, and that this little bolt was put here to prevent any of the inmates of the house from

disturbing him or his ' pals ' without warning.
Mr. Beresford thinks the same, and recom-
mends you to leave the bolt, but to take
away the catch, so that any intruder wishing
to make himself secure may draw the bolt
without noticing that there is nothing to
hold it."

With a knife Gerald took out the screws,
feeling rather glad for once of the torrent of
talk with which his old friend whiled away
the time spent in this cold bare outhouse,
where the noise of gnawing rats was heard
under the stones, and the lamp, which Mr.
Shaw talked too fast to notice, smoked, and
flared, and made ugly flickering shadows on
the whitewashed walls. Mr. Shaw was a
man of strong sense, but of almost equally
strong prejudices, and he made full use of the
opportunity this eventful visit to France
afforded of comparing the insecurity of property
under a Republic with the ease and peace of
mind he enjoyed in his own home in loyal
Streatham.

" Don't talk to me of liberty and fraternity
and equality," he said, glaring angrily up at

Gerald's coat-sleeve, as the young fellow twisted out the screws. "Give me a country where any rascal isn't at liberty to help himself to the contents of my pockets, and to walk in and out of my back door as an equal, and help himself to the contents of my brotherly larder. In Streatham, thanks to the Queen," Mr. Shaw was in too great a hurry to be severely logical, "I can go into my scullery at any time I like, without fear of meeting anything more alarming than a blackbeetle or a burglar, neither of whom has the right to resent my appearance. But here, good Lord! I suppose if poor Beresford were to come upon a couple of his free-handed equals regaling themselves on his cold mutton, or hiding under the sink a few thousand pounds' worth of property which we in England should call stolen, they'd think nothing of blowing out their intrusive brother's brains."

Gerald laughed as he pulled out the last screw and came down from the wooden chair, and Mr. Shaw took him by the arm and continued more seriously : " You must come back

to England, Gerald, where, at least, if there
are some rogues about, they are not considered
the equals of honest men. I was very glad
to see there was nothing to attract you about
that little pale nonentity of a girl: it was
rather wicked of you to tell her father she
was beautiful ; even the 'prentice of olden
times would hardly have steeped himself in
such flattery as that."   Gerald fidgeted, but
said nothing.   " However, we'll find you a
good berth either in my office or a better one,
and you shall find a good wife in your own
country—handsome too, don't be afraid, for
I'm not so sure after all that the ugly ones
are always the best."

He turned away and walked round the
great bare echoing outhouse as he talked, and
it was not until the end of a speech which
contained much shrewd but rather obvious
moralising on the advantages and disadvant-
ages of beauty in women that he found, on
returning to the kitchen-door, that Gerald
had slipped through it.   Attracted by the
sound of a closing door, Mr. Shaw followed
him through the kitchen, the sound of his foot-

steps being deadened, as Gerald's had been, by the piece of matting which was laid across the stone-paved floor. Hearing a girl's voice in the passage, he stopped short and took the liberty of eavesdropping.

" Who's Babette ?" said the girl's voice sharply, though in a low tone.

" Oh, nobody—at least, nobody *you* need mind," answered Gerald, in a voice quite different from that he had used to Mr. Shaw. " Look here, I've brought you the chocolates, but somebody put a beastly heavy bag right down upon them in the *carriole*, and they're all squashed up."

They both laughed in subdued tones, and the girl said " Thank you," as if taking something.

" I did so wish you were here to-day," she continued softly. "I had such a lovely breezy walk down by the sea, and saw a lot of rabbits popping in and out of their holes. It's a beautiful place—if it wasn't for my father ; I don't like him at all."

" Hush ! you mustn't say that—it isn't right."

"I don't care——"

"Be quiet; I won't hear you say such things. Now go upstairs: I hear your father moving; he is coming out."

"I'm afraid to go upstairs, when they've been talking like that about robberies and things; you don't know how it frightens me."

"Don't be silly. Go, they're coming. Good-night, good-night."

Mr. Shaw heard a light tread upon the uncarpeted polished stairs, and he entered the passage just as the girl's black skirt was disappearing at the turn of the staircase, and Mr. Beresford, leaning on the housekeeper's arm, opened the door of the *salle-à-manger*.

"Well, have you taken the bolt off?" said Mr. Beresford to Gerald, who was still standing at the foot of the stairs.

"Yes, sir."

"I have been telling Mr. Beresford," broke in the housekeeper's wiry precise little voice, "that it is my firm opinion that the robbery in the train was committed by the same persons who have been making this

neighbourhood the scene of their depre-
dations."

"This opinion, though it has certainly not
much proof, is scarcely reassuring to quiet
country folk living two miles and a half from
the police-station," said Mr. Beresford rather
gloomily.

Mr. Shaw, who looked as grave as he,
hesitated for a few seconds before speaking,
which was a most unusual circumstance with
him; then he said very quietly:

"If Miss M'Leod should prove to have
made a good guess, I don't think our fears
about the safety of 'Les Bouleaux' need
be of long duration. For I have a clue to
the perpetrators of the robbery in the train
which, though of no value in my hands,
will in the hands of the police as surely
lead to the discovery of the person who
actually took the notes from Blair's pocket
as if the thief was already branded with
the crime."

"What—what is it? Why didn't you
give it to the police at Calais?"

"I shan't trust to them; I am going to

Paris to see the head of the police department."

"You are very wise," said Mr. Beresford, with more respect than he had hitherto felt towards the talkative Englishman. "But take my advice; put yourself under police protection for the journey, in case your appearance on the line again should be watched for. And now good-night, for I think, though you are a strong man, and I am only a weak one, you must be nearly as much fatigued as I am. I heartily wish you a good night's rest."

And they all went upstairs and separated for the night. Miss M'Leod had given up her own room to the visitor, as it was larger and more comfortable than the spare room. But no comfort, no luxury could have made Mr. Shaw sleep that night. Thoughts of his old friend Staunton, of that friend's unlucky son, and of the unfortunate Blair, kept him tossing through the remaining hours of darkness.

"I wish I hadn't come here at all," he thought to himself, as the gray of a dull morning began to glimmer through the blinds. " I wish I'd gone straight back to Paris, and seen poor Blair out of his difficulties, before thinking about Gerald. I could have got more rest in the train than here. I couldn't feel less like sleeping if it were my last night on earth."

CHAPTER II.

On the morning after the robbery in the train, dawn broke very cold and gray over "Les Bouleaux." It was the end of March, but the north-east winds were still keen, and they cut straight along the barren sandy coast, and altered the shape of the sand-dunes, sweeping beautiful smooth surfaces on the sides of some, till they looked like frozen waterfalls, filling up hollows at the foot of others, and bearing gritty blinding little clouds along to choke up what scrubby vegetation the winter had spared. The poplars and birches that grew thickly round the house and garden swayed and cracked drearily, as if tired out under the efforts of the blast, which had already kept them in violent motion some hours, when Mr. Shaw, after a short sleep which refreshed him but little, pulled aside one of the neat muslin blinds of the window nearest to the centre of the house, and looked out.

Rather a pretty garden it was in summer, with a very undulating little lawn surrounded by tall trees, and sloping down to a small and rather ill-kept pool, where gold-fish were supposed to live. But whenever it rained at all heavily, those unintelligent pets used to make off into a little stream which any rise in the waters brought over a depression in the path; and a day or two later, their dead bodies would float back into the untidy fringe of grass and rush and weed that bordered the little pool.

On the sandy path that skirted the lawn at the other end of the garden, Mr. Shaw saw a small black figure walking slowly along, with face upturned to watch the cracking poplar-branches above her head, and with a certain air of obstinate enjoyment of things that might have excited admiration on such a bleak and bitter morning. He saw her turn to penetrate the tangled wilderness of trees and dead brushwood that shut in the garden at the end, when a young man ran out from one of the tree-hidden paths that skirted each side of the lawn, and Mr. Shaw turned away from the window impatiently. He was a practical man, inclined to look upon any sort of love-making as a waste of energies which might be employed in reading improving books or in mastering some useful science, fortified by which, a young man, arrived at an age when he wanted some one to pour out his tea and mend his clothes, would be in a fit state to choose a partner for life with calmness and discretion, and would be able to slip into the married state so composedly and rationally that, on his wedding morning, he would not forget, on going to church, to take his umbrella with him.   But devotion which would bring a man flying out, with his coat unbuttoned, on a bitter March morning, was unreasonable and absurd.

Gerald came up with Miss Beresford as she was stooping over the tiny leaves of some wild anemones, whose fragile little buds were waiting for the tardy sunshine to unfold them.

" What have you found ?" said he.

Light in her eyes and colour in her face—
that was the answer he got, as she rose up
and shook hands with him.

"Aren't you cold?"

"No. I came out as early as I could,
because it's such a lovely place, and there
is such a lot to see and find out everywhere."

He looked at her in surprise. "Lot's to
see! Why, there's nothing but sand and
poplars!"

"Oh yes; there are little streams winding
all through the woods, and I've seen rabbits
running about; and then there's the sea only
a little way off. And do you know, I've
found a swing!"

"Yes; that's been here ever since anybody
can remember. You must let me try it first,
if you want to use it, for fear the cord should
be rotten."

So they went a little further along the
path, till they came to a clearing among the
trees on their right hand, and there stood the
old swing. Miss Beresford let her companion
try it, and then she placed herself on the

seat, and let him swing her, as happy as a child.

"I should like to stay here all day," said she exuberantly.

"You had better not let Mr. Beresford hear you say that. He has a high idea of his own dignity, and I should think he would have a still higher one of his daughter's. He would like you to be just like Miss M'Leod. And so," he added rather mischievously, "would the Fourniers."

She stopped the swing the next moment, as her feet came near the ground, looking suddenly grave and rather cross.

"I thought they were your friends, and you liked them!"

"So I do, and they are my friends. But old M. Fournier isn't the sort of friend you would race down a hill for a franc. And Madame and Mdlle. Fournier won't walk on the grass, for fear of getting their feet wet, and are very careful of their complexions."

"And—and the *other* M. Fournier?"

"Victor?"

"Yes."

"Oh no, of course he doesn't care about his——By-the-bye, though, I think he does take care of his complexion too. And I think he would be a little shocked by a lady who didn't take care of hers."

"That's all right," burst out Miss Beresford, with great relief. "Then he won't like me."

"But how will that be 'all right'?" asked Gerald, bewildered. "Surely when you are going to marry a man it is better that he should like you?"

"Why, of course, if he doesn't like me he won't want to marry me; and as I've made up my mind not to marry him, the sooner we come to an understanding the better."

She announced this decision in a bright and easy manner; yet something in the girl's tone reminded Gerald so strongly of her father when he had gone through the portentous process of making up his more important mind on any subject, that he looked at her for a few minutes in a rather helpless fashion without making any remark.

"Don't you see?" she added, smiling, and

perfectly satisfied with the decision at which she had arrived.

"Oh, ah, yes, I see what you mean," he answered slowly. "But to hear you talk like that about 'will' and 'won't' is quite funny to anyone who knows your father as well as I do. Besides, only the night before last you were humble and submissive, and, knowing quite well why Mr. Beresford sent for you, you were ready to fulfil his wishes. And now you talk like a different person."

"Because I *am* a different person," said she quietly; and as she looked up, with pink colour in her cheeks and little wind-tossed curls all in disorder above her eyes, he thought so too. "I'd been leading such a wretched life, you know," she continued pleadingly. "Poor mamma didn't care for me much; she looked upon me rather as an expensive lady's-maid, very handy with her fingers, but entailing, through my unfortunate relationship to her, a shocking outlay in fares, and in boots and gloves. The rest of my garments didn't cost much, as I made them myself out of her old ones; but she was always lamenting that she had to give them to me before they were worn out."

"Why did you stay with her, to be treated like that?" asked Gerald indignantly.

"She couldn't have got on without me, for one thing; when you've been in the habit of scolding the same person every day for twenty-one years, you would miss that person dreadfully. Besides, I was so used to it, that when two or three hours passed without her finding fault with me I thought she was ill."

"Don't talk like that—I can't bear to hear you talk like that," said Gerald, pained and bewildered. For all the time she spoke the tears were coming nearer and nearer to her eyes. "It's over now, and I dare say she was sorry at the last. It must have been a dreadful life, though!"

"It was worse, afterwards, to feel that I belonged to nobody. Then I had to think about earning my own living, and I felt that it was a degradation, which was silly; and I also felt that I didn't know how, which was worse. I hated my father for leaving me like that. I wouldn't be a governess, because I

19—2

wouldn't teach what I didn't know, as all we
poor half-educated ladies are obliged to do.
So I began to learn the harp, to play at
concerts."

"Are you very fond of music, then ?"

"No, I can't bear it. I would rather have
been a shop-girl, but it is very difficult to be
a shop-girl. It's very difficult to be anything
at all if you're a woman. So when my father
wrote and proposed that I should be a wife, I
thought I had better accept the situation—or
at least apply for it. But since I wandered
about this place yesterday all by myself
among the trees and the sand-hills, the
beautiful wind seemed to carry away some
of my bad thoughts and bring me some good
ones."

"What bad thoughts did you have ? I'm
sure they were not really bad, only a little
strange because you've had such a strange
life."

"Oh yes, they were bad. It was very
mean of me to let myself be shipped over
here so meekly, when all the while I didn't
intend to be meek unless I was satisfied with

my bargain. But now I've made up my mind to go to my father and tell him that I'm very sorry I ever consented to come, and that I'll go back to England, and will never trouble him in any way again. I feel a sort of new energy in me since yesterday, and I see that it is a great deal less degrading to earn one's own living than to allow one's self to be offered for sale; especially," she added, with a considerable diminution of haughtiness, "when one feels that one is not likely to prove an attractive bargain."

"Oh, but that doesn't matter," said Gerald, with rash haste. "I mean," he went on, as she looked quickly up at him, "that Victor has left the matter in the hands of his father, and he had every reason to believe you had done the same. He would consider himself bound to carry out the contract in any case, and bound also to do his best to make you happy, I am sure," he added honestly.

"I wonder why my father wants me to marry him?"

"I don't know. Nobody ever knows why Mr. Beresford wants anything, but he always gets it. You see, he is so very clever, and so superior to everybody else, that he feels that other people's thoughts and beliefs can't be of any consequence compared to his."

" Why, that is just selfishness."

" Oh, I don't know. Clever people can't help seeming selfish, I suppose; and he has been very kind to me."

Thus easily shirking a difficult question, Gerald, seeing that Delphine was making elaborate gesticulations at the window of the *salle-à-manger*, took Miss Beresford's arm in his, and made her run with him as fast as her feet and his could take her back to the house. Mr. Shaw was waiting for breakfast; and Delphine, as she threw open the French window, told Gerald, in what she meant for an undertone, that monsieur had been watching him, and had not looked pleased; so that the three sat down to breakfast feeling some constraint.

" I suppose Mr. Beresford never appears as early as this, Gerald ?" said Mr. Shaw, when they had all been munching almost in silence for some minutes.

" No, he comes down at eleven whenever he is well enough, and has his breakfast when Miss M'Leod has hers. I'm obliged to have mine at nine, because I have to be at St. Pierre by ten."

" Then I'm afraid I shan't be able to see him before I start, for I want to get to Paris as quickly as I can about poor Blair's business, and I have to see Madame de Lancry first."

" Madame de Lancry! About Mr. Blair's business ?"

" And about—yours."

The men exchanged looks of trust and intelligence which caused Miss Beresford to glance from the one to the other with jealous curiosity; but they said no more upon the interesting subject, and remained preoccupied with their own thoughts to the end of the meal. They had scarcely risen from table when old Pierre brought in a note written by Miss M'Leod, but dictated by Mr. Beresford, begging Mr. Shaw not to go until the sender of the note had seen him; therefore Gerald had to start alone for Calais, though it was with great reluctance that he shook his old friend's hand at the hall-door.

"What time are you coming to Calais? I should like to see you again at the station," said Gerald eagerly, as he got up into the gig and took the reins.

"I can't tell how soon Mr. Beresford will let me go; but I shall be off as soon as I can. I feel that more depends on to-day's work than we know of, and I have more than a curiosity to hear what our excitable friend the Roman empress has to say."

"Madame de Lancry? What she said about my father has been ringing in my ears ever since. I shan't be able to rest till you have seen her. She seems to think she can explain such a lot of things."

"Too many. A specific for toothache only one might try before rushing to the dentist; but one that professed to cure cramp and lumbago as well would be mistrusted by every intelligent sufferer."

"Then you expect nothing from Madame de Lancry's revelations?" asked Gerald, in a disappointed tone.

"I can hardly say that. To tell the truth, she impressed me more than seems quite reasonable. I almost think if she had had a flat nose and irregular teeth I should have set her down unhesitatingly as a lunatic; but as it is—— Well, I wouldn't recommend *you* to have anything to do with her, or she may prove more dangerous than if she were one. She is very handsome," he said, with decision; "she *may* be very good," he added, with doubt; "but there is something wrong with the face—take my word for it."

Gerald listened dutifully, though his old friend's words scarcely had the effect of destroying his interest in the beautiful lady who had professed such an attractive sympathy with him and his fortunes. He told Mr. Shaw that he would most carefully sift anything he might hear, and that he would try to be back early in order himself to drive his friend into Calais after all.

As the gig rattled away over the stones of the courtyard, and Mr. Shaw turned back into the house, he found little Miss Beresford at the door of the *salon*, looking at him with

the sort of half-defiant, half-frightened expression one can imagine on the face of a very
big rat brought suddenly face to face with
a very small terrier. " Shall I fight or shall
I run away ?" That was what the look said ;
and Mr. Shaw decided the question by opening
the *salon* door for her and following her in.

" You and Gerald seem very good friends
already," said he.

She took this as a challenge, and answered
at once : " Yes, and you want to prevent him
from being my friend, when he's the only one
I've got." And though she held her head in
the air and spoke with considerable acrimony,
her eyes and nose grew red and her lips began
to quiver.

" Well, well, you see it won't do for either
of you to interfere with your father's arrangements, Miss Beresford. You would both
suffer, and Gerald the most. I am told that
your father has promised you to the son of
his partner, and in that case I don't think
you ought to play with the feelings of a poor
lad who could never aspire to marry the
daughter of a rich man."

" But who says he does, Mr. Shaw ? He's only known me since the day before yesterday, and I'm not so handsome that it is impossible for a dear nice boy like Gerald to run about the garden and the hills with me without falling in love with me."

" No, I don't say you are," said he frankly. " But, you see, there are no other girls about, and under those circumstances—without any disparagement of your attractions, Miss Beresford—a little beauty goes a long way."

Miss Beresford stood looking out over the grey-green wintry lawn into the trees beyond with a disconsolate and rather humble expression. Then she said, in a weak wistful little voice : " I like Gerald."

" Of course you do, and therefore you wouldn't like to get him into trouble with your father, would you ?"

" No-o, I shouldn't like to get him into anything that would hurt him."

And Mr. Shaw perceived, as she raised a mournful little face wistfully, submissively to his, that this independent young person had quaint little charms of manner which might

prove exceedingly perilous. He was on the
point of speaking to her more leniently when
the door opened, and Mr. Beresford came in,
leaning on Miss M'Leod's arm, and holding
a telegram and a letter.

When the first greetings were over, he sat
down and addressed his guest.

"I am sorry to say," he began, handing
the open letter to Mr. Shaw, "that from this
report, sent me this morning from the _bureau_
de police at Calais, the robbery seems more
mysterious than ever. You know that the
train was very full, that every compartment
was entered at Calais, and the passengers
questioned before they were allowed to descend.
Well, it seems each passenger denied that any
persons left the carriage in which he or she
travelled while the train was in motion : so it
is suspected that one compartment must have
contained a whole gang of thieves, in which
case, of course, concealment of the stolen
property would be easy enough, though the
chances of ultimate detection are greater. I
would most strongly advise you, Mr. Shaw,
not to travel on that line to-night—if it is

still your intention to go to Paris—without
an escort of police."

"I dare say you are right," said Mr. Shaw,
looking grave as he read the letter. "The
beggars must be clever enough for anything,
even to know what business takes me back to
Paris. By-the-bye, I must find out the time
of the next fast train. I must not lose any
more time."

"There is a good one at seven to-
night——"

"Oh, that is too late; I——"

"One moment, I beg," interrupted the
paralytic, with the haughty courtesy of an
autocrat unaccustomed to have his will dis-
puted. "I will tell you my reasons for
suggesting that time. An English clerk of
mine, a very clever fellow, who sees most
things that go on round him without taking
the trouble to look, chose for me the compartment in which you travelled last night, and
must therefore have stood near it to prevent
other passengers from getting in and taking
the remaining two corners. I telegraphed for
him very early this morning, and he is sure

to be here this afternoon, probably by the
train that leaves Paris at 9.40 and gets into
Calais at 2.41. He cannot be here before
half-past three, and then we shall have to tell
him the whole story, if he hasn't picked it up
on the road, and question him as to the people
who came near the compartment before the
train left Paris last night, between the time
you and Mr. Blair left your rugs in it to go
to the buffet, and the time Miss M'Leod and
myself got in. As soon as we have heard
what he has to say, Gerald shall drive you
into Calais, as I think I understood you to
say you had a call to make in the town before
starting on your journey."

"Yes, yes, that is so," said Mr. Shaw,
who felt bound to acquiesce in his host's
arrangements, which were indeed good ones,
although he was impatient to be in action,
remembering the haunting misery on the face
of the unlucky Blair.

It did not seem to occur to the autocratic
Mr. Beresford that anyone should venture to
interfere with plans which he had condescended
to make, and his eyes turned towards his

daughter almost before Mr. Shaw's words of hesitating acquiescence were out of his mouth.

" You will want some new dresses, Margaret," he said solemnly, " for I am most anxious that you shall make a good impression upon M. and Madame Fournier on your first introduction. They will probably call without delay ; therefore you must go into Calais with Miss M'Leod to-morrow ; her taste and judgment will be useful to you. Should the Fourniers' formal call take place before you are dressed as my daughter should be, you had better keep out of the way."

" I will, you may be sure of that," said the girl, crimson with mortification at having to listen to such an admonition before a stranger, yet not daring, after all her bravado in his absence, to defy him in his presence.

She sat rigidly for a few moments, trying to keep back the tears ; then, mad with shame and anger, she jumped up, rushed to her room, put on her shabby ulster and travelling hat, and ran downstairs and out of the house, to fight down in the open air

the storm of angry passions which convulsed
her. At first this proceeding answered beauti-
fully. She wandered away through the
straggling wood which she had traversed with
Gerald on the evening of her arrival ; she
crashed through the long broken-down dead
grasses and the bending osiers, crossed paths
which would be green and soft in summer,
passed tiny pools made by the winter rains.
And she jumped across a brook into a long
field, where an old pony was grazing who
tried to kick her. And she got between the
bars of the fence at the opposite side, and
found herself among the barren, sandy rabbit-
warrens which stretched down to the sea.
Here she felt the north-east wind in her face,
and walking was difficult ; for the uneven,
yielding ground was covered by short brownish
grass and brambles, and by a thick growth
of rushes whose net-like roots caught her
feet as she stepped ; and the whole surface of
the sandy earth was honeycombed by rabbit-
holes, in and out of which the little creatures
popped as she went by.

The keen air and the smell of the sea which

came to her over the great stretch of yellow smooth sand which lay between the warrens and the frothy edge of the waves as they rolled in, brought back her colour, her spirits, her sense of independence : she roamed about by herself until the dull March sky began to grow dark towards evening; and then, suddenly frightened, although she would not have owned it, at the idea of what her father would say to such a long and vagabond ramble, she turned her face towards the house and ran at full speed. All went well with her until she had got over the warrens and into a field she did not know, at the other end of which was the wood which enclosed the house and the gardens. It was getting dark under the trees as she reached them, and she was too much excited and was running too fast to be very cautious : just as she came under the bare branches she saw that a stream—the same she had already crossed higher up—ran between the field and the wood. It was narrow, but its banks were steep and slippery. She tried to draw back, but too late ; the moment after she had

discovered the water she was in it, narrowly
escaping an entry head-foremost.

To sneak and to scramble out, wet to the
knees, bruised, scratched, muddy, and miserable, was comparatively easy : to find her
way through the wood to the house was not
difficult, but to get into it, and to slink
upstairs unheard, unseen, was work for a
heroine indeed.

There was a carriage in the courtyard.
She dared not go to the front door, she
could not get in at the back door ; so she
crept round to the other side of the house
and reconnoitered, tearful and shivering.
There was no light yet in the middle *salon*,
and the window was ajar : here was her
opportunity.   She darted along the path,
flung open the window, and was in the room
like a whirlwind.

There for a moment horror kept her still.
For there were little cries at her sudden
appearance and some commotion and alarm.
Near the stove sat Mr. Beresford, whose weak
eyes made him always reluctant for the
artificial light to be brought until the daylight

was quite gone. The unlucky girl saw also the faces of Mr. Shaw and Miss M'Leod. But besides this sufficiently awful conclave there were two visitors—a stiff and tall old gentleman, a voluminous and erect middle-aged lady. They both looked at her well, at first not at all understanding who she might be. But Miss M'Leod's horror-struck exclamation : "Miss Beresford !" betrayed the secret. And poor Peggy, as she rushed wildly across the room and slunk out at the door which Mr. Shaw mercifully opened for her, knew that she had just had the honour of making her first appearance before her destined father and mother in law, M. and Madame Fournier.

CHAPTER III.

Poor Peggy felt, as the door of the *salon* closed behind her and she crept with downcast head along the hall, as if the last faint inducement to continue to exist had gone. How could she now, after this desperately humiliating, degrading, and irredeemable introduction to her father and mother in law elect, go proudly to her father as she had intended to do, and, with all the maidenly and womanly dignity at her command, inform him in an eloquent speech that she had determined, rather than let herself be sold to a man she did not know and (this taken for granted) could not care for, to return to England, and, renouncing the brilliant prospects he had held out to her, earn for ever after an obscure but independent livelihood? She couldn't renounce anything now; she could only wait meanly to hear the announcement, from her father's cold, unsympathetic lips, that she was a failure, and that the position of his acknowledged daughter was an honour too great for her to bear.

As she sneaked along the hall, blind and deaf to everything but her own unspeakable humiliation, she suddenly felt a hand laid gently on her arm just when she had passed through the doorway which led to the stair-case. She started with a low cry of nervous terror. It was only Gerald, who was looking kind and sympathetic. He had just returned from Calais, and was taking off his driving-gloves.

"What's the matter, Miss Beresford?"

"Oh—Oh—Oh! Everything's the matter. I—I fell into the water, and M. and Madame Fournier, and—and my father and everybody saw me—all—all over mud! Oh, why wasn't it dee-e-ep enough to drown me!" sobbed she.

"Who is it? What has happened?" asked in French a bright man's voice unknown to her.

She turned her head and saw that the last, worst blow of all had fallen. By her side, looking down at her with much amused astonishment, was a tall, slight, handsome young fellow, a little too showily dressed for an English gentleman, who was twirling a very small dark moustache into neat upturned points, and smiling serenely as if it were the only possible expression for one's face when looking at a woman.

" Mdlle. Beresford ?" he asked, still smiling, with his head inquiringly on one side, as he examined the limp, crushed, shabby little person of his future bride.

" May I introduce M. Victor Fournier ?" said Gerald hastily, in a coaxingly gentle tone, which caused the bridegroom-elect to look at him with raised eyebrows, but without relaxing the chivalrous duty-smile.

It was such an informal ceremony altogether, this ghastly finale to a most ghastly incident, that Victor, after making a deep bow which she answered by a drooping and despondent curtsey, good-naturedly held out his hand, and received, on the lavender glove he wore for this ceremonious call, the impress of three muddy little fingers. She saw at once what she had done, but by this time her despair had reached the point of recklessness, and she looked up at him with the solemn face of one for whom misery has exhausted its terrors.

" I am very sorry I have spoilt your glove, monsieur," she said, in slow, halting French; " but you will forgive me to-morrow, when I have left this horrible place."

" Not horrible so long as mademoiselle remains here," said Victor readily, with another bow, bravely keeping up the smile in the face of circumstances. " I have the pleasure to hope that this desolate place will long be enlivened by mademoiselle's presence."

The idea of her presence enlivening any place just now was such an unmistakable joke that Peggy looked up with a forlorn little curl of the lips which was meant for a smile. Gerald, who felt that the situation was becoming every moment more awkward, and who was afraid that she might burst either into tears or into a fit of equally disconcerting laughter, suggested that she had better run upstairs and change her wet boots, and gave her a little fraternal push towards the staircase.

" Adieu, monsieur," said she, with a strong British accent, bowing to Victor.

" Au revoir, mademoiselle," said he, bending low to her.

And Gerald thrust his arm through that of his friend, and led him back to the *salon*, while Peggy went up to her own room, and began pulling off her wet ulster with a defiant determination to take her final departure from " Les Bouleaux " in it as soon as it was dry. There was consolation in the thought of speedy action, and before she had wrenched off her soaking, spoilt little boots she had begun to sing aloud to herself in a tuneless, uncertain sort of manner, to indicate that despair had driven her to a policy of insolent, open defiance ; that, in short, she was going to run away from " Les Bouleaux," and they might catch her if they could. She was quavering out the first verse of " The Vagabond " for the third time, when a sharp, precise little rat-tat sounded outside her door.

" Who is it ?" she called out in the " Vaga-bond " manner.

" It is I, Miss M'Leod," said a thin voice. " Can I come in, Miss Beresford ?"

Miss Beresford limped across the waxed floor with a scowl on her face, unlocked the door, and admitted the visitor haughtily. Miss M'Leod was haughty too, and being even smaller than the younger lady, she had to tilt back her head to a very painful angle in order not to be outdone in the matter of superciliousness.

" I have come, by Mr. Staunton's desire, to inquire whether it is your intention to descend to the *salon* previous to the departure of M. and Madame Fournier and their son, and whether, in that case, I could afford you any assistance in the matter of preparation for the interview."

And Miss M'Leod trifled with her eyeglass in would-be easy condescension.

" No, I've seen quite enough of them. If my father sent for me, you can tell him I sha'nt come."

The housekeeper raised her eyeglass, and

returned the girl's furious look by a vacant stare of her little light eyes which was meant to express contempt. Then she turned, and was sweeping towards the door, uttering voluble and unheeded assurances that she had never been treated in such a manner before, and that Mr. Beresford should be informed of the uncouth impertinence to which she had been subjected, when, as she turned again towards the girl with a final denunciation, her indignation was checked by a sudden sense of the piteousness of the shivering, chattering, bare-footed, miserable little figure before her, trying to force back her tears, and to bear a brave front, while the mud and the water still dripped from her spoilt dress, and her teeth chattered with the cold. Miss M'Leod was not really hardhearted, and she was hesitating as to what form of words she could use to reopen negotiations with dignity, when a sound of running footsteps was heard in the corridor, and then a knock at the door.

At first neither lady moved or spoke in answer. Then there was another knock and they heard Gerald's voice.

" Miss Beresford! Margaret! Peggy!" he cried imploringly. "Come out and speak to me—come to the door. Do, *do!*"

Miss Beresford rushed to the door and let her face appear at a one-inch aperture.

"Oh, Gerald," she cried, in vehement reproach, "why did you send this woman up to me? Don't you think I'm miserable enough? *Do* make her come out, *do* take her away."

Gerald thrust his hand through the crack, and Peggy instantly put her fingers into his to show she had forgiven him.

"Miss M'Leod, what have you been saying to her? Kiss her, tell her you didn't mean to be unkind, and help her to dress as quickly as ever you can, as you promised," said he, with eager volubility. "You know you said you'd lend her something to wear. And, Peggy, do be good, there's a dear girl, and dress and come down and play them something, and be amusing and bright and nice and sweet, as you can be, and then it will all blow over, and I can dance at your wedding in a month after all. Say you will—quick—to please me."

He drummed and tapped on the door
affectionately as he spoke, and Miss M'Leod
took the opportunity to make conciliatory
advances on the other side; so after some
excited remonstrance on the part of Peggy,
Gerald was sent to call Delphine, who was
active if not particularly neat-fingered; and
the little housekeeper having brought from
her room a black silk dress of her own, and
some carefully folded lace, and a coral neck-
lace, she and Delphine proceeded to array the
reluctant Miss Beresford in them, and to pin
and to fold and to fasten the borrowed garments, until Peggy, as she was led out into
the corridor where Gerald was anxiously
waiting for her, looked like a rather pretty
little stage Puritan, in a dress which was
very short for her in front and very long
behind.

" Now you look lovely," whispered Gerald,
with honest admiration, as he allowed Miss
M'Leod to pass them down the stairs, and
followed with Peggy's arm held tightly in
his; " and Victor will be delighted with you,
and it will be all right. Mind you don't

fall," he added tenderly—he didn't know how tenderly—making her walk slowly down the stairs and noting her appearance with much pride. "You don't know how wretched it made me to see you look so unhappy; and I felt I would have done anything, *anything* to make it all right again for you."

And they stopped at the foot of the stairs.

"Oh, Gerald, you are a dear good fellow," said Peggy gratefully, squeezing up one of his hands in both hers, and looking at him with penitent affection. "You've made everything seem different; you've made that little snappish Miss M'Leod angelically good to me; and now I feel quite clean and happy and not a bit afraid of those dreadful Fourniers. And I will try to please them—to please you. You're just like a brother to me, indeed you are!"

So he took the fraternal privilege quite simply and naturally, and was surprised and a little hurt when she shrank back as he kissed her cheek.

"Are you angry? Don't be offended with me. You would let your brother kiss you."

"I—I don't know," said she rather shyly.
"Nobody has ever kissed me before."

Gerald had nothing to say to this, but he
believed it; and it gave him a great deal to
think about afterwards. He lingered there
with her for a moment, until a loud, obstru-
sive, chuckling laugh above their heads made
them both look up, to discover Delphine
craning her neck over the top of the staircase
till she was blue in the face, to get a good
view of them.

"Come along, Peggy," he said hastily.
And he crossed the hall, and opened the *salon*
door, and whispered, "Mind you play well,
and be as bright as you can," as she, with her
heart beating very fast, and a terrible feeling
of the awful conduct she had to atone for,
passed him, and went into the room.

Miss M'Leod had already heralded her reappearance. And she looked so modest, so
fresh and charming, with the bright colour
brought by shame and excitement to her
cheeks, and the humble pleading look in her
eyes, as her father, after a mollified glance at
her, introduced her formally to M. and Madame

Fournier, that the remembrance of her first
bird-like entrance only served to enhance the
good impression she now made by her gentle
self-possessed manner ; and Madame Fournier,
a good-natured, honest, commonplace Flemish
woman, whose *dot* had been her chief attraction
in her husband's eyes when he married her,
but who had since acquired boundless empire
over him, drew the girl towards her in a
motherly manner to which she was quite
unaccustomed, and asked if she could look
upon her as upon the mother she had lost.

Peggy looked straight into the lady's kind
eyes, while the tears gathered slowly in her
own. "Yes," she then answered simply ;
and Madame Fournier gave her a hearty kiss
on the forehead, mistaking the girl's hesitation for a natural feeling that no one could
quite take the place of the mother who was
gone.

Mr. Beresford noticed the good impression
his daughter was making ; Gerald grew quite
joyous over it ; Victor, indifferent as he was,
seemed relieved by the change in his bride-
elect. The stiffness of the ceremonious call

was lost in the singularity of the circumstances
which attended it, and the former conclave
had grown into a most harmonious gathering,
when a new arrival suddenly checked the
chattering tongues and laughter, and brought
back the thoughts of the whole party from
love and marriage, and such comparatively
cheerful subjects, to robbery and outrage.
Yet the intruder looked good-humoured
enough ; and it was only the remembrance of
the gloomy circumstances which had caused
him to be sent for which cast a cloud upon
the assembly as plump little Mr. Smith, with
his round black head and twinkling black
eyes, walked briskly into the room.

In the pause which followed his greetings
the Fourniers rose to take leave ; and when
Mr. Beresford, who had not yet recovered
from the fatigue of his long journey from
Nice, took advantage of their departure to re-
tire to his own room as the lamp was brought
into the *salon*, the rest of the party, left to
themselves, gradually became silent listeners
to Mr. Smith, who was characteristically
already in possession of a theory about the

robbery which was ingenious, though not without weak points. The theory was that the robbery had been arranged and carried out by the servants of the railway company, one of whom had entered the compartment at Paris while he himself was standing by it; and he suggested that it must have been the guard himself who, accustomed to walking the length of the train while it was in motion, to examine the tickets, according to French custom, had availed himself of this accomplishment to execute the robbery his accomplice had prepared. The weakest point of this theory was the difficulty of suggesting any means by which the servants of the railway company could have learnt that Mr. Blair had a very large sum of money about him, a fact which was only known to Lord Keighley, Mr. Shaw, and perhaps to M. de Breteuil.

The theory, such as it was, served for discussion until the appearance of another visitor, M. Durand, curé of the parish, a devoted admirer and adherent of Mr. Beresford, whose philosophy he took as a joke, and whose lavish charity he held up as an evidence

of true religion, which, while saving the soul
of the donor from infernal torment, preserved
the bodies of his poorer co-parishioners from
the pinch of cold and hunger—a trial which
the simple-minded curé was not spiritual
enough to underrate. He, too, had to hear
the story of the railway robbery, and he
differed altogether from the ingenious Mr.
Smith and the practical Mr. Shaw, being
inclined to attribute the misfortune boldly to
supernatural agency.

"Our unhappy country is most clearly ac-
cursed during these latter years," said the
old man, whose eyes, shining brightly out of
his worn, parched, and shrivelled face, burned
with the fires of strange beliefs picked up
among the peasants, whose friend and servant
he had been so long. "France is suffering
for the sin of rejecting her kings and insulting
her Church. Both these institutions are of
God, and can it be wondered at that when a
nation casts off His service it should fall
under the dominion of the devil?"

"But the devil can find no use for bank-
notes ; and, if he could, he is clever enough

to make forgeries that would be cashed at any bank," said Mr. Smith.

Miss M'Leod looked shocked, Peggy interested; Gerald watched Peggy, and Mr. Shaw wished that this well-meaning old simpleton had remained at home with his breviary.

"The devil delights in making useless mischief, in doing evil for evil's sake," said the curé dogmatically. "He has plunged us in war, in compulsory education for minds which do not cry out for knowledge, in starvation for bodies which do cry for bread. He has, they say, during the past winter taken bodily shape to plague the miserable inhabitants of this very district. What more likely, then, than that this fresh outrage, diabolically planned, diabolically carried out, leaving no clue, admitting of no solution, was the work of the Prince of Darkness himself?"

A short silence, during which the rest of the party glanced at Mr. Shaw, as if expecting him to take up the challenge; but, fond of talking as he was, he apparently felt that

to talk about clues to a man like the curé
was beneath him.

It was Gerald's fresh young voice which
broke in after old M. Durand's gloomy tones :
" I don't know about the devil, but I know
somebody who is mixed up in this business,
or at least in part of it; and that's old
Monnier, the gamekeeper."

Mr. Smith and M. Durand were rather
astonished by this blunt and decided assertion;
but the account of his seeing a stranger at
the cottage, and of the utterances of the little
boy whom he had found in the wood on the
evening of Peggy's arrival, was listened to
with attention by them.

" Perhaps Babette would account for the
stranger," suggested the blunt Smith.   But
Gerald's anecdotes had made some impression
upon him, for when a rather rambling discussion of the alleged apparitions in the
neighbourhood had gone on for some minutes,
the English clerk rose abruptly and said he
would go to Monnier's cottage at once, and
try to surprise or frighten either the gamekeeper or his daughter into a confession, if

they had anything to confess. The little man himself seemed rather nervous, and as he rubbed up the spectacles through which he was wont to boast he could see into a difficulty as a hawk into the night, Gerald noticed that his face was moist and that his little fat hands were trembling.

"Hallo, Smith!" cried the young fellow. "Are you funking the walk down the avenue for fear of seeing the black stranger and his attendant wolf?"

The curé silenced him by a look and gesture of such horror that everybody in the room was uncomfortably impressed by it.

"These are not matters to be laughed at," said he solemnly and sternly. "Whether the apparitions which have frightened the peasants are real or imaginary, I myself can vouch that their reported appearance has never failed to be followed by calamity to somebody."

Curiously enough, the person most affected by this speech was Mr. Smith. He tried to hide the fact, and nodded to Mr. Shaw, telling him he should be back in time to

drive him into Calais, in his usual genial
voice. But he was not himself; and as the
rest heard him cross the hall, go out at the
front door, and slam it violently after him,
Gerald laughed, and suggested that the sturdy
little clerk was not quite so strong-minded as
he liked to be considered. But the old cure's
superstitious earnestness, without affecting
their reason, had depressed the spirits of all
his hearers; Mr. Shaw began to grow restless,
looked constantly at his watch, and said that
he should like to start as soon as possible.
Miss M'Leod begged him to have tea first,
and led the way into the _salle-à-manger_, where
the table had been spread for him by her
orders.

He was much touched by her kindness,
and as he sat down he said, looking at
Gerald, who had followed them into the room,
that he was glad to leave the boy in the kind
care of such a friend.

"Friends," chirped the little lady, correct-
ing him; "it is not I, but Mr. Beresford,
whom Gerald has to thank for everything."

"I don't know about that," said Mr. Shaw

slowly. He was looking grave and thoughtful, and an unusual intensity in his manner arrested the attention of both his hearers. "The kindness of a shrewd philosopher ought perhaps logically to be considered of more value than that of a simple-hearted woman. Yet in the long-run I shouldn't wonder if Gerald decides that he owes more to you, who mend his stockings because he has nobody to do it for him, than to Mr. Beresford, who metaphorically pins him to a piece of cardboard as an interesting specimen."

Gerald looked surprised, but Miss M'Leod was indignant at the implied disparagement of the autocrat of " Les Bouleaux."

" If you knew Mr. Beresford better," she said, with dignity mitigated by a pleasant sense of over-praised modesty, " you would know that his heart is just as warm as if he were only an ordinary man."

Mr. Shaw said nothing to this, but went on eating toast in a dogged manner which implied that his opinion was unchanged. Gerald offered him everything on the table affectionately, and watched his old friend with an ever-increasing reluctance to see the last of him. When he rose and went into the *salon*, where Peggy was finding the entertainment of the curé, who was rather deaf, a dull task, Miss M'Leod left the room to tell Mr. Beresford that his guest was going. It was nearly half-past five, and as the train to Paris started at seven, and Mr. Shaw had to call on Madame de Lancry before that, there was no time to be lost. He shook hands with Peggy, who was rather bewildered by the events which had affected her that day, by the sense of the importance of Mr. Shaw's mission in Paris, and by the knowledge that there was some mystery about Gerald in which this Madame de Lancry was concerned; and the next moment the door opened, and Mr. Beresford came in, leaning on the arm of the little housekeeper.

"I could not let you go without making an effort to come and bid you good-bye," said he, as he sat down in his large carved arm-chair by the stove, and held out his hand to Mr. Shaw. His manner was rather less dry and reserved than usual, and it was with some human warmth of tone that he gave his departing guest a few shrewd instructions as to his treatment of the Paris police officials, with whom his errand would bring him in contact.

"Above all, do not let your clue, whatever it may be, go out of your possession except to the head of the department himself," he said. "If you cannot see him at first, I think, considering the grave nature of the case, you might call at the British Embassy, and ask for the intervention of the Ambassador himself to get you an interview. And now I will not detain you, for I know you have a call to make in Calais, and you have not much time."

Mr. Shaw thanked his host, shook hands with him, with the curé, and then turned to Miss M'Leod.

"I hope I may have the pleasure of seeing you again before very long," said he, as he pressed her little thin dry hand warmly. "I am sorry not to be able to say good-bye to Mr. Smith ; he promised to drive me into Calais, but he has not come back yet, and so———"

"Oh yes, he has come back," interrupted
the housekeeper acidly, "but not in a fit state
to drive anybody, I'm afraid. I met him upstairs just now on his way from Mr. Beresford's
room to his own, and——"

"Hush, you mustn't tell tales," interrupted
Mr. Beresford indulgently. "The *cabaret* at
the end of the avenue is a little too near, and
poor Smith's tastes are a little too convivial.
As long as my business doesn't suffer from
his pleasures I excuse him. He will be all
right in the morning, and a good deal ashamed
of not having kept his word to you, poor
fellow."

Mr. Shaw excused him readily enough, and
left the room, accompanied by Gerald and by
Peggy, who had made up her quarrel with
him. They were all three crossing the hall
towards the front door, which was open, and
through which they saw the *carriole* standing
ready in the courtyard, when the big Delphine
came clattering from the kitchen like a
charging dragoon, and seized Mr. Shaw with
muscular grip, her round rosy face convulsed
with terror.

"Monsieur, monsieur, don't go to-night; wait till to-morrow, do, do wait, or some misfortune will happen to you, sure enough! It will indeed. Ask M. le Curé. He knows; he will tell you you must not go."

"Don't be silly, Delphine. What is it you mean?" said Gerald uneasily.

"Oh, M. Gérald, the wolf has been seen about to-night! It means ill-luck; tell monsieur not to start to-night."

"What a silly girl you are, Delphine!" said the young man, as he pushed her aside to follow Mr. Shaw, who was already outside the door.

Standing on the stones of the courtyard, with the feeble light from the little lamp over the hall-door shining on his kind grave face, on his gray moustache and beard, he was waiting for Gerald to come out, and looking at him affectionately. Peggy, who was watching him, suddenly slipped down the steps and put her hand again into his.

"Do you believe in those superstitions of the old priest and of Delphine?" she asked, in a rather frightened whisper.

" No, my dear, not a bit. Do you ?"

" No-o, not exactly—at least, I mean of
course not, not at all. But still I wish—I
wish you weren't going to night ; I should
like you to stay a little longer, now I know
you are so kind, and such a good friend to
Gerald. The fact is," she burst out, in a
different tone, excitedly drawing his hand up
to her breast and looking at him anxiously,
" all these mystery and robbery stories have
made me nervous and silly, and—and—you
are sure you'll be safe, aren't you ?"

" My dear child, whether the train will or
will not carry me quickly and safely to Paris
is my only care. Of wolves, in the flesh or
in the spirit, I have no fear at all, I assure
you. Gerald, my boy, we really must not
linger any longer."

He shook the girl's clinging hand again ;
the young fellow tore himself away from the
excited Delphine ; and both gentlemen got
into the *carriole* and drove off.

Just as the clumsy little carriage left the
stones of the courtyard for the sand of the
avenue, Peggy, who was watching it fade

into the darkness, was startled by a voice behind her. She turned quickly, and saw her father standing in the doorway, leaning on Miss M'Leod's arm.

" Do you think you could catch them up, and tell them to drive fast, as fast as they can ?" he asked, with earnestness most foreign to his usual dry, hard manner.

" I—I'll try," stammered Peggy. And she sped out over the stones along the soft avenue until she came up with the *carriole* just as it turned into the high road.

Both men were startled by a breathless voice which broke upon their ears as the little face looked up at them. They were sitting in the front of the *carriole,* side by side.

" Drive, drive fast, very fast, as fast as you can !" panted she, in a voice shrill and broken with excitement and exertion.

And before they could stop the fat old horse, the little sibyl had dropped behind them, and was lost to them in the darkness of the avenue.

CHAPTER IV.

As Peggy Beresford's little elfin face disappeared behind the hood of the *carriole*, Gerald instinctively reined in the fat old horse, which he had been at some pains to worry into abnormal speed. But Mr. Shaw, less susceptible, touched the lad's arm reprovingly.

" She has good reason for what she says, you may be sure. Drive fast. Perhaps her words were a message. At any rate, I have no time to lose."

Gerald's face grew suddenly hot, and he whipped up the horse with great energy. This valiant attempt to cover an emotion which his companion had not even noticed was the more unnecessary as it was already dark—not with the darkness of night, but with the gloom of the cloudy close of a sun-less day. There was no moon, but they could see the light-coloured sandy road which lay for some distance straight before them, with flat bare fields on either side, and nothing but an occasional clump of leafless poplars or a tangle of dead bushes to break the monotonous stretch of uninteresting landscape between one group of cottages and the next. Gerald would have liked to talk, but the preoccupied manner of the elder man had to be respected, so he whistled softly to himself to while away the time until Mr. Shaw should think fit to break the silence. This the latter presently did upon the very subject which, in spite of the mysteries about his father and about the recent robbery, which had filled his mind all day, was at the moment first in Gerald's thoughts.

" An odd little girl," Mr. Shaw said slowly.

" Odd ! Who ?" asked Gerald, knowing perfectly well who the odd little girl was.

" Miss Beresford. It isn't a woman and it isn't a child, and it isn't a demon—at least, I don't think so ; but it is a little of all three, and—I like it."

"Why do you say 'it'?" asked Gerald shyly, not liking to show that he was offended, though his whole heart was in arms.

"Because to say 'she' would be to do the queer little caricature of humanity great injustice."

"Caricature!" exclaimed Gerald indignantly. "Why, she's very pretty."

"Ye-es, in a way. But it is a wild weird sort of prettiness that made her, in my opinion, look ten times better when she dashed into the *salon* all over mud, with her hair half-down behind, and falling into her eyes in front, than when she walked soberly in, all washed and combed like Miss Brown or Miss Robinson, and tried her hardest to be exactly like anyone else."

"Well, I thought so too," Gerald admitted with hesitation. "But I didn't expect you to say so, Mr. Shaw. I thought you liked girls to be what is called well-behaved, with their hair combed away in front, you know, and coiled into a little knob like a shell behind—like Miss Brown or Miss Robinson, in fact."

" So I do ; in most respects the ordinary well-combed girl is infinitely Miss Beresford's superior. But you can admire a wild rose as well as a garden rose, though the one has a commercial value and the other hasn't. And while I admit I should be sorry for the persons to whom this young lady stood in the relation of wife, housekeeper, or mother, and I doubt whether she will ever be even tamed down into an agreeable hostess, yet she is shrewd and amusing *en tête-à-tête*, and when left to herself she is picturesque. As she made that sensational entrance, though she looked half like a scarecrow, she looked half like a fancy picture of the north wind. I wonder what in the world that unlucky young Frenchman will do with her !"

" Unlucky ! Victor !" stammered Gerald, amazed and incautious. " Why, he ought to be standing on his head with delight."

" If he indulged in such pranks as that he would be a better match for her, certainly," said Mr. Shaw imperturbably. " And their household would at least be lively. As it is,

I can't help thinking they stand a poor chance of happiness, as far as one can see."

"If—if I thought that——" began Gerald, in a low, husky voice.

But he did not say what he should do if he thought that. Mr. Shaw turned to look at him, but did not ask him to finish his sentence; and there was silence for some minutes, until they passed a man who was coming in the opposite direction. A lean and bent eld man he was, dressed in the usual blue blouse of the working class; he was walking quickly, and did not glance up as the travellers passed. Gerald leaned out of the *carriole* to look after him; there was not light enough to see much, but the man's shuffling, halting gait was unmistakable.

"Why, it's old Monnier!" cried the young fellow. "He has been into Calais to-day, I suppose. Then Smith didn't find him at his cottage, so of course that's why he turned into the *cabaret*, as he's too fond of doing. I wish he had come with us; he's so jolly clever and so popular everywhere, that you would have travelled twice as comfortably if he had said a word or two to the guard and the station-master. He can nearly always manage a side of the carriage to himself, no matter how crowded the train is."

"That was not altogether an advantage last night," suggested Mr. Shaw thoughtfully. "On the whole, I am glad Mr. Smith has not come."

"Don't you like him? Mr. Beresford thinks very highly of him."

"Yes; I could see that."

Something in Mr. Shaw's tone puzzled the young fellow, who looked curiously at him while he said:

"Of course, you didn't see enough of him to find out how clever he is; but I assure you in business he is Mr. Beresford's right hand."

"I should say he is more than that : he is Mr. Beresford's brain."

Gerald was too much amazed by this start-lingly heterodox statement to have anything to say in refutation of it. He looked from his companion to the animal he was driving, and wondered by what strange chance such a

22—2

shrewd man of business as Mr. Shaw had
failed to be struck by Mr. Beresford's hitherto
unquestioned superiority to everybody else.

" You don't like Mr. Beresford : I can see
that, sir," he said diffidently, after a silence.

" To be frank, I do not." The flood-gates
were open at last, and the elder man turned
towards the younger with almost a sigh of
relief. " It is not a gracious task to have to
speak against the man whose guest one has
been within the hour to another man who is
his guest still. But since half-truths are dangerous, and you are by your position deeply
interested in the character of this man, I will
tell you my opinion : it is, that Mr. Beresford,
philosopher and philanthropist, is nothing but
a selfish hypochondriac, with just sense enough
to get himself well served, and to know that
the less he says and does himself, and the
more he leaves to his clever clerk, the better
it will be both for his interests and his reputation. The clerk knows this as well as the
employer, and profits by it, no doubt : he
probably has a good deal of business on his
hands of which his paralytic employer knows

nothing; but, rogue as I believe him to be, I confess I prefer his audacious knavery to the cold-blooded cynicism of the other."

" What do you know about Smith ? What have you found out ?" asked Gerald, deeply interested. " You must know something to speak like that."

" Well, yes, I do. I learnt by chance, whilst in Paris, that this trustworthy Mr. Smith is making private bargains of his own with one of his employer's clients."

" Impossible ! Who was it with ?"

" With M. de Breteuil."

" M. Louis de Breteuil ? One of our best clients. I must tell Mr. Be——"

" You will do nothing of the kind—yet. You only know enough to bring yourself into disgrace with both of them, for Mr. Beresford would believe nothing against his confidential clerk without strong proof. And all I can tell you at present is that I myself, when I accompanied Blair on his second call at M. de Breteuil's hotel, heard the open-faced little Smith say, as he and the millionnaire passed me on the stairs, that ' a bargain made with

an old paralytic didn't matter much, and would
not interfere with their agreement.' And they
both seemed to enjoy the joke immensely."

"I wish you hadn't told me; it has made
me feel so jolly uncomfortable," said Gerald,
after a pause.

"And a good thing too. I don't want you
to be comfortable here; I don't want you to
stay here. You must come back to your old
friends in England, and we'll soon put mysteries and knaveries and elfin girls out of your
head——"

"No, Mr. Shaw," Gerald broke in very
decidedly. "It's awfully kind of you, and I
know it seems beastly ungrateful of me to say
no ; but I do mean to stay in this country for
more than one reason. The first is, of course,
that I must discover how and by whom my
father was murdered. The second——"

The second reason was not so easily explained, for the young man stopped.

Mr. Shaw nodded disapprovingly.

"Of course—the elfin girl!"

"It's not exactly that," said Gerald apolo-
getically. "At least, not—not in the way

you mean. But, you see, the poor little thing has got no friends, and her father doesn't seem to care for her much, while—while she and I, you know, seem to get on very well together, not like—like spoons, you know—not a bit like that, but more like chums, you know. She isn't stiff, like other girls, at least not with me—I mean," he corrected himself hastily, "she's only stiff before strangers, you know."

"And how long is it since you were a stranger to her?"

"Well, of course—er—two days isn't really a long acquaintance; but then, when people meet first in a rather unceremonious fashion, without having anybody to introduce them to each other, why, I think they seem to know each other quicker."

" I've no doubt they do."

"I don't see the use of such a lot of fuss about formal introduction, myself. It seems to set up a barrier at once between you and the person you're introduced to; just as if the introducer said, 'I know I'm doing a risky thing in introducing to you such a bad character as this ; but there—I'll hold myself responsible for his decent behaviour.' If Mr. Beresford had formally presented me to his daughter, as M. Fournier did to Louise, I should have looked upon her as I do upon the Dresden figures in the cabinet in the drawing-room, pretty silly things too fragile to play with, and whose value I don't understand. But when you first meet a girl curled up in a chair like a kitten, with her head hanging down over one side, and her little feet stuck up in front of her on a level with her shoulders, you—you—er—why, you feel she isn't china. And—and that's how I feel about Peg—Miss Beresford."

" Well, I think it's a great pity Peg—Miss Beresford wasn't formally presented to you by her papa. It's a mistake in the long-run for a lad to see so few young women that he looks upon them as china ; but when once he has got to look upon them in that light, it is better he should continue to do so, and, above all, that he should not want a Dresden figure for his own cabinet."

" But, Mr. Shaw, you're not a bachelor."

" No, my boy ; but no right-minded martyr would wish to send others to the stake."

" And yesterday you said if I came to England you would find me a nice wife."

" Yes, but not the promised wife of another man. Gerald, take care what you're doing ; for if you interfere with Mr. Beresford's plans, you will find——"

He stopped, and peered out from the hood of the *carriole.* Gerald's glance followed in the same direction, but he saw nothing except a bit of straggling hedge that bordered the roadside for a little way, up to the rough wall of a dilapidated and deserted cottage some hundred yards in front of them.

" What was it ?" The circumstances of the drive, the subjects of their thoughts, were just gloomy enough for both men to feel a suspicious interest in every animate object about them.

" I thought I saw something running on the other side of those brambles."

" A rabbit, I expect ; the ground all round here is honeycombed with their holes."

" It was a rabbit four feet high, then."

" A donkey, perhaps."

" Very likely."

Neither of the men made any attempt to resume the interrupted conversation. Both kept their eyes upon a turn of the road still some yards off, where the ruined cottage on the left hand, and a copse of small trees and bushes on the right, closed in the prospect. Gerald gave the old horse a smart cut with the whip, and, at the moment the animal began to quicken his pace, a low whistle was distinctly heard from the direction of the copse.

" Hullo !" said Gerald softly, glancing at his companion, who gave a short nod to intimate that he heard, and swung his legs over the front of the *carriole* for freedom of action in case of emergency. For, without exchanging a word on the subject, both men had prepared, during the last few minutes, for foul play of some sort. As the *carriole* was drawn rapidly into the shadow of the tangled branches, the younger tightened his hold on the reins, glanced round at his friend, and their eyes met—for the last time.

"There is something wrong, I am sure of it. Shall we turn back?"

"No. It is too late. Drive on—fast."

Again Gerald drew the whip sharply over the horse's now steaming flanks. There was something in front of them, some dark object crouching by the side of the road, on the right hand, nearest to the side where the young man sat. The latter had scarcely caught sight of it when the low whistle was heard again, and Gerald knew that the crouching object was a man. With his eyes steadily fixed upon that spot, he turned the whip in his hand to have the butt-end ready for defence, when suddenly he felt the shock of a heavy weight flung with force on to the front of the *carriole* and a roaring furnace breath against his neck, while the gurgling sounds of a beast in fury fell upon his ears, and Mr. Shaw's loud cry of "Help!"

He was only just in time, as he turned, to see his friend dragged down to the ground by the jaws of a great animal, whose long white fangs and red bright eyes shone in the darkness. He was springing up to help him when he felt the horse, which had been checked by the attack and by the fall of Mr. Shaw, stop short; the two-wheeled *carriole* fell back with a jerk, and just as Gerald was thrown backwards over the seat into the interior of the vehicle, he saw a man, whom even in that rapid glance he could see to be very tall and very slim, spring from the horse's head towards him. A moment later, as, half stunned by the violence with which his head, in falling, had struck against the back seat of the *carriole*, Gerald was trying to scramble up to the help of his friend, he felt a long cold hand upon his throat, and looking up, he saw quite plainly even in the darkness the face of his assailant. Only for a moment; as, with struggling breath and starting eyes he lay helpless, with a hand at his throat and a knee upon his chest, meeting with horrible, involuntary steadiness the steady gaze of the man whom he believed to be his murderer, noting on the instant every feature, freezing under the frigidity of the pitiless eyes, he felt himself suddenly blinded, then gagged, and lastly bound, still with the cries of his old friend ringing in his ears, still making frantic efforts to get free.

He knew that he had no hope of escape; knew that the long cold hands were quick and skilful, and that the infinite torture he was suffering as he lay blindfolded, expecting every moment to feel the muzzle of a revolver against his temples, was the work of very few minutes; but the sense of his own danger was deadened by a strong conviction that he was only a secondary victim, that however it might fare with him, it would fare worse with Mr. Shaw. As well as he could, for the handkerchief which was tied tightly across his mouth, he made broken entreaties, gasping out such words as came first, in the agony of his heart.

"For God's sake—don't hurt him—don't hurt the other man! He—he is my best friend—he is goodness itself. If you are in want, he'll help you—I know he will, I swear it. For God's sake—don't—don't touch him, don't, I say——"

But the man never paused in his work, never spoke. Having bound Gerald's arms to his sides, his feet to each other, he leapt down to the ground, as the young fellow knew from the tilting forward of the _carriole_. For a few seconds, whether there was silence or whether he was partly stunned by this last rough jerk, Gerald heard nothing. Then Mr. Shaw's voice, clear, loud, and strong, rang out in tones that the young man never forgot :

" I _know_ you !"

Then followed a sharp crack of the whip, which the assailant had wrested from Gerald as he attacked him ; and the _carriole_ went jolting and jerking over the rough road at a speed it had never travelled before, the scared horse galloping on in the dark, while Gerald in vain tried to free his hands from the cord which bound them, and to reassure the horse by the tones of his voice, which were, however, changed and muffled by the handkerchief tied across his mouth. The _carriole_ had been dragged some hundred yards before Gerald heard any further sound but the thud of the galloping horse's hoofs and the creaking and bumping of the vehicle. Then above all these monotonous noises his straining ears caught a cry that froze his blood and checked his breath, and made his shuddering body cold and wet as he fell back again, inert and despairing, on to the floor of the carriage.

For the voice was that of Mr. Shaw, and the cry was " Murder !"

On went the *carriole,* rumbling and rocking; the old horse, his flesh still quivering from tho unmerciful and unaccustomed lash, galloped along the well-known road towards Calais, with foam-covered bit and steaming flanks. The road was straight, flat, and little frequented; there was no obstacle to turn aside the frightened animal, no solitary foot-passenger to stop him until he drew near to the turning on the right hand which led into the town of Calais. Here the canal runs alongside the road, separated from it by a wooden fence and a strip of rough ground. A group of loitering *gamins* shouted and yelled at the horse, attracting the attention of some workmen on the bridge over the canal, two of whom came running towards the corner when in the dusk they descried the grey-covered top of the old *carriole,* as it came swaying and shaking towards them. As the *gamins* followed in a yelling, hooting flock, the horse, whose pace had grown slower from exhaustion, made a last frantic effort, and, dashing up to the corner with an instinctive attempt to make the accustomed turn, brought the off-side wheel in such sharp contact with the post and rails which fenced off the field by the canal from the road that the *carriole* was over-turned and the shafts snapped like tinder, leaving the old horse free, but so effectually checked that he was easily caught by a lad, while a group of those who had witnessed the accident gathered round the fallen vehicle.

" Some one inside !" cried one man, as he peered under the partly shattered cover.

" He is hurt !" " He is still !" " He is dead !" cried different voices, as men and boys swarmed, pushing and peeping, about the overturned carriage.

Then a voice rose in authoritative tones above the rest: " Stand back, keep off the *gamins*. If the man is breathing still, he will not breathe much longer if you crowd over him like herrings and keep off the air."

And two or three strong-armed workmen forced back the foremost of the growing crowd, while the man who had first spoken, aided by another in a blouse, opened the door of the *carriole* and gently drew out Gerald's prostrate and senseless body. At the first sight of the handkerchief with which he was gagged, now wet and blood-stained, and of the cords which bound his arms, murmurs and exclamations broke from the nearest onlookers; their cries were taken up by those behind till the road was in an uproar; men, women, and children struggling, screaming, and running, some to get the best possible view of the backs of those persons who had been lucky enough or muscular enough to get close to the wretched carriage, some to meet the police, who were hurrying to the spot.

"There has been a crime!" "It is a murder!" were the whispers, the cries, that ran like wildfire from mouth to mouth, while those about the senseless man cut the cords which bound him, and did their best to revive the not yet extinct life within him. By this time he had been recognised, and his name

was repeated with redoubled sympathy for
him, with redoubled horror at the crime of
which he had been the victim. For Gerald
Staunton and the gig and the fat horse were
well known in Calais and St. Pierre; and
though he had few personal acquaintances
outside the factory, his good-humoured face
and his evident disgust at the turn-out he
drove had made him a familiar and popular
feature of the neighbourhood.

At the first sign he gave of returning consciousness, he was, on the suggestion of one
of the workmen from the factory who
happened to be among the throng, carried
on an impromptu stretcher straight into the
town of Calais and to the house of M. Fournier, where the strange story caused the
utmost consternation among the family, who
were at dinner when the unconscious guest
arrived.

He was taken up to Victor's own room,
where motherly Madame Fournier tended him
herself, while Louise, after being refused permission to see him, went into hysterics in the
dining-room. When the young man opened

his eyes he at first remembered nothing, but stared silently at the green curtains of the bed on which he had been placed, and smiled at the kind face of the lady bending over him. It was not until he caught sight of Victor, who was standing behind his mother, looking very grave and anxious, that Gerald's face clouded with dull pain and perplexity. The young Frenchman could not restrain his eager solicitude : at this first gleam of intelligence in his friend's eyes he leaned over the bed-side, and asked impetuously :

" Gerald, who was it attacked you ?"

The young fellow suddenly sprang up on the bed, with fire in his eyes.

" He has been—murdered !" he cried hoarsely.

Madame Fournier fell back in bewilder-ment and horror ; Victor pressed past her, and supported the young fellow in his arms.

" Who—who has been murdered, Gerald ?" he asked, in tones almost as hoarse as those of the injured man.

But Gerald's head sank wearily, and his eyes grew dull and gentle again.

"Who!" he repeated, trying to rouse himself; "why—why, it was my father! No one will believe it, I know; but they did murder him. Can't you let me sleep now? I will tell you the whole story in the morning."

Victor laid him gently down, and turned to his frightened mother.

"Poor fellow! His head is not quite clear yet," he whispered.

He was retreating from the room, when his mother rushed towards him and seized his arm.

"Where are you going, Victor? What are you going to do?"

"I am going to ride to 'Les Bouleaux' to inquire into this."

"No, no; you must not go to-night—while there are robbers, murderers about," said she excitedly, clinging to him.

He disengaged himself by a deft movement, and addressed her from the passage with a more dramatically valiant air than an Englishman would have thought necessary, but with earnestness and fire.

"What one man can dare another can, mother. I will not rest until I have done what I can to discover who committed this crime!"

Before she could utter one word more, he had shut the door and hurried down the stairs.

CHAPTER V.

VICTOR FOURNIER rode to "Les Bouleaux" as fast as his English horse, which had long been the envy of the less fortunate Gerald, could carry him. He was sincerely anxious to find out who it was that had used Gerald so ill, curious as to what had become of Mr. Shaw, and just sufficiently interested in the queer little English girl whom he was to marry to feel glad that her father's house was to be the scene of his inquiries.

Delphine opened the door, and showed the ingenuous surprise of a rustic servant at sight of him. He had fastened his horse to the garden-paling on the opposite side of the courtyard, to save time, and he now stepped quickly, and without speaking, into the hall, whip in hand.

"Monsieur desires to see Mr. Beresford?" inquired Delphine, looking at him curiously, as she began to cross the hall towards the *salon.*

"Wait a minute," said he, stopping her. He did not wish to give unnecessary alarm, and he thought the girl might supply him with some of the information he wanted.

"Is Mr. Staunton at home?" he asked tentatively.

"No, sir. He has gone to Calais with the English gentleman who came last night."

"Mr. Shaw? Are you certain of this?"

"Yes, sir. I myself saw them drive off in the *carriole;* I was standing at the door here with Mr. Beresford, and Miss M'Leod, and *la petite demoiselle,* who ran after them to tell them to drive fast, by her father's desire."

"To drive fast! Mr. Beresford said they were to drive fast?" cried Victor excitedly, seizing the girl's strong arm, and peering with intent eyes into her face. "Were they late, or was he afraid of something? Speak out, can't you?"

But the girl began to call upon the saints

and to implore the Virgin to protect them all, with irrelevant devotion which made the young man stamp his foot impatiently.

At last she exclaimed in a loud guttural whisper : " The wolf! I know it is the wolf! O, what has he done ?"

" Be quiet a moment," said Victor authoritatively. Then, having decided that the best person to ask for was the clever English clerk, he went on, " Where is Mr. Smith ?"

" He is in bed, sir. He went out this afternoon soon after you and M. and Madame Fournier had left ; he returned a little while before Mr. Shaw and M. Gérald went away, but he had been drinking ; so Mr. Beresford, who met him on the stairs, told him to go to bed," answered Delphine, aching with curiosity and alarm, but constrained by Victor's commanding manner to confine herself to replies.

" And Mr. Beresford ? Is he in bed yet ?"

" No, sir. When the gentleman had gone, he and Miss M'Leod went back to the *salon*, where he has been ever since, playing chess with M. le Curé."

Victor paused a moment, considering what he should do. Then he glanced at the door, and saying, "I will go in," he followed Delphine, who burst open the door with alacrity, and clattered over the polished floor of the first *salon*, which was empty, to the entrance of the second.

"M. Victor Fournier!" she announced in a loud hoarse voice, shaking with excitement; and then she drew back to allow the gentleman to pass her, and watched the effect of his entrance without ceremony from the doorway.

Everyone looked up in surprise. Mr. Beresford, with a pawn in his hand, peered up from the chessboard under the green shade he wore to protect his eyes from the glare of the lamp; the curé, his opponent, who was sitting opposite, with his back to the door, turned and examined Victor over his spectacles. Peggy and Miss M'Leod, who were sitting near the fire, the former nursing her chin, the latter knitting, both uttered exclamations of alarm, and listened to his vehement words spellbound with horror.

"Mr. Beresford—ladies—*mon père*," he burst

out in fiery haste, his eyes travelling rapidly from one to the other, "I have bad news—I do not deny it—you can see it in my face. I fear—I know—that a crime has been committed!" Miss M'Leod screamed, and Peggy started up and leaned against the mantelpiece. "Gerald has been hurt—and Mr. Shaw——" He paused, but no one could speak to tell him to continue.

At last Mr. Beresford signed to him to go on, with a trembling hand.

"Mr. Shaw is missing."

Not the charitable curé, not either of the tender-hearted ladies, was it whom these tidings utterly overwhelmed. It was the philosopher, the cynic, Mr. Beresford, who sank back in a heap into his chair, muttering low cries of horror, crushed and appalled by the awful news.

"I warned him—I did warn him—my God, I did!" they heard him mutter hoarsely to himself, as he bent his grey head upon his hands and shook with anguish which astonished all the rest, even at that moment of general consternation.

Victor crossed the small room to him, and reverently touched the old man's clutching, quivering fingers.

"Don't give way like that, Mr. Beresford. It may be all right. We don't know anything yet. It was only a wild guess of mine; it was stupid and mad of me to tell you. Mr. Shaw may—must have got out of the *carriole* before it reached Calais. He will probably have turned up safe and sound by this time, and——"

But, raising his head, the old gentleman interrupted him in tones that no one present ever forgot:

"No, no; he will never turn up. He has been murdered!"

Peggy sprang forward, in the midst of the awful hush which followed these words, and clung to Victor's sleeve.

"Oh, tell me, tell me," she begged, in a voice so broken that the young man could scarcely understand her—"Gerald—Gerald—is he—murdered too?"

Victor shuddered.

"No; he is quite safe at my father's house,

mademoiselle. And so, I hope, in spite of
Mr. Beresford's fears, is Mr. Shaw also by
this time."

He turned, and saw that the master of
" Les Bouleaux " had risen from his chair,
and was standing, supported by his faithful
housekeeper, who was unmistakably in tears,
shaking as with palsy as he tried to cross the
room towards the door.

" Where are you going, sir ?" asked Miss
M'Leod timidly through her tears.

" I—I must go upstairs. I—I must see
Smith," said he, in a voice that sounded
strange and broken.

" But he is asleep, and he was not sober
when he went to bed. He won't be able to
help you," she persisted, her tone growing
rancorous at once.

" He knows something—he guesses something," murmured the old man, as the others
made way for him. " He said something
about Monnier when he came in, and I met
him and told him to go to bed. I must see
him at once."

The two went upstairs as fast as Mr.

Beresford's infirmity would allow, and after knocking some moments at the door of the spare room where Mr. Smith was sleeping, at last a drowsy voice called, " Come in !" and the housekeeper left her employer to go in, and returned to the *salon* below, where Peggy was sitting, rigid and dumb with horror and distress, on a low chair by the fire. Victor was watching her with curious eyes which saw more than the pale little face before him, and the good curé, with professional instinct, was improving the occasion by an unheeded homily on the ways of Heaven.

The young man started forward on the entrance of the housekeeper.

" They are upstairs together—Mr. Beresford and Mr. Smith ?" asked he hastily.

" Yes ; they are in Mr. Smith's room. You must not go—you must not intrude," she added in alarm, as Victor passed her.

" I must and will know all they know—all they can suggest," said he resolutely.

And without waiting to hear more objections, he left the room, went upstairs, and, turning to the right, walked along the corridor until he came to a door on his right hand which stood ajar, and through which the weak flame of a candle threw a line of light before his feet. He could hear two voices—the one firm and hard, the other alternately piteous and angry. The former was that of Mr. Beresford, who, having partially recovered his own self-control, was trying to induce the clerk to do the same.

" Come, be a man, Smith, be a man," he was saying as Victor drew near the door. " I've been a good master to you—not too strict in the matter of perquisites, not too hard upon occasional excess. Pull yourself together for once. My very honour is concerned in this awful business—Mr. Shaw was my own guest. For God's sake leave off snivelling your wits away; dress yourself, go back with young Victor——"

" May I come in ?" asked the young man, who had now reached the door, and who was losing patience with the half-audible tipsy objections of the clerk Smith, whose cleverness when sober was only equalled by his imbecility when drunk.

He gave almost a howl as Victor's voice startled him. Mr. Beresford, more collected, though even his nerves were not proof against a start at the interruption, said, " Come in."

Victor entered, grave, handsome, earnest. He glanced from the stupid-looking bullet-headed Smith, who was sitting in his night-shirt on the edge of the bed, childishly sobbing and wiping his eyes with a crochet mat, to Mr. Beresford, who, while scarcely less affected than the other, had by this time got enough command of himself to bear the horrible catastrophe with dignity as well as grief.

" Victor," said the latter, turning to the young man, " you're a good fellow, a brave fellow, to have come back along this road in the face of what might have been danger for you too. But you shall not go back alone; since this coward will not stir, I will go with you myself, old and infirm as I am, and, with Heaven's help, we may find Mr. Shaw breath-ing yet."

With a sudden jerk, more like a mechanical toy just wound up than like a man stung into heroic resolution, Mr. Smith bounded off the bed and began to dress, complaining piteously and vaguely that "it was just like his luck." Victor gave Mr. Beresford his arm, and they left the unhappy clerk to shake and snivel himself into his clothes as quickly as he could. Outside the door the young man said suddenly :

" You talk of hope, Mr. Beresford, but I can see that you feel none. You have some theory about this horrible affair."

" Yes, I have; but I warn you that, instead of explaining, it makes the outrage more mysterious. Whether poor Mr. Shaw has been killed or not, I do not know ; but I believe he has been attacked and robbed by the thieves who have haunted the Department this winter. It's a very terrible thing, this ; it points to there being a regular organized gang in the neighbourhood, to whom no one is sacred; and if they attack people in carriages, Heaven only knows whether before long they may not try their hands on us in our own homes !"

For the selfish fears which checked the current of the older, colder blood Victor had little sympathy: he willingly made over his companion to the cares of old Pierre, who, more helpless than ever in his horror at the story Delphine had brought into the kitchen, gave a trembling and untrustworthy arm for his master's support. The young man had scarcely reached the bottom of the stairs when Smith, still maudlin, but rather more coherent, overtook him, and linked his arm, for sympathy and steadiness, within that of the young Frenchman.

"If we must go corpse-hunting along that beastly road, let us have the priest with us, if it's only for company," muttered the clerk, directing his companion's steps towards the *salon.*

Smith had been brought up a Roman Catholic, and although he had impulsively professed a variety of creeds since that, and had never been particular to a dogma or two, he still occasionally carried his sins and his remorse to the confessional, and took spiritual guidance when nothing better offered.

The curé, though not physically fearless, was far too good a man to shrink from any

call which might be taken for that of duty,
and he at once consented to accompany them
on their search for any trace of Mr. Shaw.
Victor turned back and slipped into the inner
salon for a farewell word to Miss Beresford,
whom he still found sitting looking blankly
and forlornly into the dying fire. He was
very much in love with Madame de Lancry,
and an officer's daughter with the manners of
an officer's son ran this lady a good second in
his admiration ; but his heart was a gallery
where room could always be made for a new
picture, and the young English girl who was
to be his wife, with her piquant face and odd
freedom of manner, might on sufferance be
accorded a place there. The faithful Miss
M'Leod had gone upstairs, dutifully to worry
her employer. Victor had mastered the interesting fact that English girls were allowed
a great deal of liberty with their *fiancés :* why
should he not take advantage of these circumstances to administer to the fragile-looking
little lady the kiss of consolation ?

There is something so dignified in sorrow
quietly borne that Victor instinctively bowed

low to her as she raised her sad eyes on
his entrance. He had not much time to
waste over his consolation, however, and he
came slowly and respectfully towards her as
he spoke.

"Pardon, mademoiselle; I am intruding,
I am afraid. I came to say good-bye."

Like a child she smiled up at him and held
out her hand.

"Thank you; it is kind of you to remember
me at a time like this."

"It is impossible not to remember mademoiselle at all times."

"You are going back now, to—to——"

"To look for—Mr. Shaw; I hope we
may find him safe."

"Indeed, I hope so too. And then——"
She hesitated again.

"Then I shall return to my father's house,
and shall see how poor Gerald is getting
on."

Her face quivered. She was standing up
now, looking away from him with a subdued,
constrained expression which he pardonably
took for the most bewitching modesty.

" Is he much hurt ?" she asked, still look-ing away.

" I hope not—I think not. He was stunned by the jolting of the cart; he will soon be all right. We'll take good care of him."

" You are very good—all of you. I am sure you will."

She looked at him gratefully, and the young man thought her tear-stained eyes were very beautiful, and wondered why his sister Louise couldn't manage to look as well when she had been crying. No opportunity could be better. Her face looked delightfully inno-cent and inviting, and her forlorn expression and attitude were not to be resisted.

" Poor little lady! You are in need of comfort too. Let me console you."

He bent his head with an unmistakable intention ; but to his astonishment, before his lips could touch her face she moved suddenly back, all the seductive limpness gone from her attitude, and most plainly expressed indigna-tion on her face. The young Frenchman's dismay did not last long.

" Why is mademoiselle so severe with me,

when she has done me the honour to accept
me for her affianced husband ?" he asked
plaintively.

"That was my father's doing, M. Fournier,"
she answered promptly.

"But mademoiselle consented to the
arrangement ?"

After a pause—"Ye-es."

" The ladies of your country are not usually
so chary of their kisses to the man they honour
with their choice."

" But there is no honour and no choice
in this case, M. Fournier; and as we have
begun the ' arrangement' in the fashion of
your country, we will go through with it
in the same fashion. M. Durand is coming
back for you. Good-night."

She gave him her hand to touch and drop,
very coolly; and Victor went away understanding much more clearly than before why
English girls are allowed so much liberty in
their engagements.

" She is a man in petticoats," he said
to himself, only half disdainfully, as he left
the house with the priest and Mr. Smith.

But she was not; she was only the ordinary little feminine fool fond of the wrong man, and therefore endowed with the stoniest strength of mind in her dealings with the right one. She went to bed unhappy about the fate of Mr. Shaw, unhappy about her engagement with Victor, but most of all unhappy because Gerald—good, kind old Gerald, whom a week before she had never seen, but whom circumstances had already hoisted into the place of honour in her young girl's imagination—was lying ill three miles away, and she could not tell when she should see him again.

In the meantime the three searchers had trudged together along the Calais road, and discovered, to their great relief, that they had been forestalled in their explorations. Distant cries and shouts were heard along the road soon after they had left the poplar avenue; and when, following the direction whence the noises came, they reached the spot between the copse and the deserted cottage where the attack had been made, they found that a party of police, sent out at the suggestion of the elder M. Fournier, who knew that Mr. Shaw was to be driven into Calais by young Staunton, had already reached it, and that a discovery had just been made which put a fatal end to all doubt about the occurrence.

For, following the marks of blood which were found in the middle of the road where the *carriole* had been stopped, which appeared also from time to time on the untidy garden-path of the deserted cottage, the police had found inside the ruined building the dead body of Mr. Shaw, with the marks of fangs at his throat, and a bullet-wound in his breast. His pocket-book, purse, watch, chain, and scarf-pin were gone, so that there could be no doubt in the mind of anyone that the object of the murder was robbery. A stretcher had been hastily formed of two boards; the body of the dead man was placed upon it, and the solemn procession back to Calais began. Victor, hastening ahead of his two companions, was the first to learn these details, the first to see this sight; then he stepped back again to inform the curé and Mr. Smith of the discovery.

The clerk, on learning it, was seized with such convulsions of horror and fright that it was with difficulty he could be persuaded to continue the walk towards Calais, where Victor had made up his mind to confront him with Gerald that night. The English clerk, though clever, had the reputation of being rather a slippery fish, and his conduct this evening had raised in the mind of his employer's son the suspicion that his drinking that afternoon, and subsequent hurrying off to bed, might have been the result of remorse, and of a wish to be out of the way of any unpleasant occurrences of which he might have got wind. So the young Frenchman was inexorable, and poor Smith had to drag his trembling and unwilling limbs towards the town, taking good care, however, to keep a considerable distance between him and the terrible freight the police were bearing in the same direction.

In turn the canal was reached, the bridge crossed, the moat and the gloomy ramparts passed, and the quiet streets of old Calais traversed, until at last, with Victor and the priest still walking one on either hand, the clerk stood before the *porte-cochère* of M. Fournier's house. Victor rang the bell, and the *concierge* opened the little door within one half of the large one, and admitted them. As they stood just inside—Smith behind the others, as he was not in a mood to assert his personality—Victor asked, "Have you heard how M. Staunton is ?"

"No better, I fear, monsieur. This lady has been unable to see him," answered the *concierge*, indicating a tall, handsomely-dressed lady, who was at that moment crossing the courtyard towards the lodge from the front door of the house.

Victor hastened towards her eagerly, crying, "Ah, Madame de Lancry! What an unexpected pleasure !"

The old curé glanced at her without interest : rich women dressed like modistes' pictures he had, through long absence from the world in which they live, ceased to regard as the possessors of souls.

But on Smith the sight of the lady, the first sound of her voice, as she begged Victor

to excuse her abruptness now, as she was
anxious to get back to her husband, acted
like a spell. He craned his bullet head
forward with one fearful stare, then, turning
sharply, he slipped through the open door,
and, seeing a *fiacre* standing there, jumped
into it, hoarsely promising the driver a
napoleon if he could drive him to the station
in five minutes.

"I've taken her own cab, I believe," said
Smith to himself, in feverish tremulous exulta-
tion, as the enterprising driver drove off at
what he considered a good pace, sacrificing
his engagements to his avarice. "Now, if I
can only get a train to Boulogne and catch
the night boat to London, I'm out of the way
of the whole boiling till I've had time to
think a bit."

But luck was against him. When he got
to the station, he found he had twenty
minutes to wait, so he went into the buffet
for a *petit verre*. He had scarcely raised the
glass to his lips when the lady whose cab he
had so unceremoniously taken entered the
room, which was almost empty, and walked

straight up to him. He did not attempt to escape her this time; he knew it was of no use.

"I thought I should find you here," she said simply, but with a certain unpleasant suggestion in her tones of an intention to "have it out with him."

"Yes—er—I—glad to see you, Madeline," said he, without much spontaneity.

"I wish to speak to you. Will you come into my sitting-room for a few minutes? I am staying here."

"Certainly, with—with pleasure. But, I say—er—Madeline, I suppose you don't want to—to have me back, or to—make it up?" said he, following submissively but coyly.

"Not exactly."

"Then aren't you — afraid of — people guessing the—the—well, in fact, that you are—were—as a matter of fact—my wife?"

"Not in the least," said she contemptuously, as she opened the door of her sitting-room, and he followed her in.

CHAPTER VI.

THE sitting-room into which Madeline de Lancry led her visitor was the same in which she had received Victor two days before. Mr. Smith glanced round him at the furniture, which was somewhat spare and unpretending, and then at the diamonds in the lady's ears, in unconcealed astonishment.

"You don't seem particularly well lodged, for such a fine lady as you have become," he suggested as an opening.

His own taste lay in the direction of plenty of glass and gilding, and he liked his colours bright.

"My husband and I find the rooms comfortable enough," said she carelessly.

"Ah yes, so you've got another hus— I mean you've married since I saw you last.

I saw it in the papers. I'm sure I hope he
—he suits you pretty well."

" Perfectly, thank you. He is an invalid,
and I only see him when I wish to do so."

" Hullo !" And Smith, who was fidgeting
round the room, stopped short and stared at
her. " You've got on, haven't you, since—
since——"

" Since you gave me my first lesson in the
duties of a wife ? Yes."

He cast at her one sidelong look out of his
round black eyes, like a convicted goblin, and
then continued his aimless promenade round
the room, while Madeline sat down in an
armchair and took off her fur cape. When
he drew near to the side of the room where
she was sitting he stopped, looked at himself
in the glass, and carefully smoothed down
with his not too clean hand a little feather-like
tuft of wiry black hair which always stood out
from the crown of his head unsubdued by the
rarely applied comb. Then he laughed with
some effort as he spoke again.

" You always were a rum 'un, Madeline,
and at the best of times one never knew where

to have you. But this beats all—that it does." And he laughed again.

"I don't quite understand," said she.

"Why, to go and marry a swell quite regular, with license and cake and everything in style, knowing all the while that there was a poor devil knocking about somewhere whom you'd promised to love, honour, and obey in Islington church half a score of years before."

He put it quite plaintively, but Madeline only laughed in her turn ; and, with some fear of a woman's foolish fancy for raking up old scores, he added quickly : " But there, I know I was a bit hasty and irritable at times —we all are, more or less ; and of course it was very natural that you should feel it, being such a fine-looking woman as you were—and as you are still, for the matter of that. And I'm not one to make a fuss over every trifling irregularity. But—but to—to ask your first husband to step in, in a friendly way, and have a chat, just as if nothing had happened, in the very house where your second husband is nursing himself in security, why—why, it shows a positive want of delicacy, Madeline, that it does."

And Mr. Smith, *alias* Meredith, pulled out his handkerchief and passed it over his forehead; for injured delicacy had made him warm.

"I'm so sorry you think that," said Madeline, leaning back in her chair, and drawing a footstool towards her. "But perhaps you will forgive me when I tell you that nothing is further from my thoughts than to talk to you 'just as if nothing had happened.' I wanted to speak to you because a lot of extremely strange things have happened since I had the pleasure of promising to love, honour, and obey you in Islington church, and because I want to know just what share you, and a certain gentleman whose name I don't think I need mention, have had in bringing those strange things about."

At the words "certain gentleman" Mr. Smith grew suddenly quite quiet, and successfully abstracted every trace of expression from his round face.

"I shall be very happy to give you any

information in my power, but I haven't the
least idea who the mysterious 'certain gentleman' is."

"Well, we won't waste any time over that.
The gentleman I mean is your accomplice,
Louis de Breteuil. Now you know quite
well that I'm not afraid of you, so what is
the use of going through all that silly panto-
mime ?" she asked calmly, as Meredith began
to dance, and to make little threatening runs
at her. "I know that you two are still
linked together ; I know that he is still living
luxuriously in Paris on the proceeds of your
combined knaveries ; I know that you have
for some years filled the post of traveller for
the firm of Fournier and Beresford in order to
veil your robberies, and to give you opportunities for more ; I know that the railway
robbery was your work——"

"Then if you know so much, what the
deuce is there you want to know more ?" interrupted Meredith, whose eyes, as round and
black and bright as a toad's, were now shining out of a moist red face, as he stood
watching her cruel face in terror.

"I want to know why Mr. Shaw was murdered."

"Good gracious!"

The very mildness of this exclamation, in the face of such a terrible implied accusation, was an emphatic protest against the injustice of it.

"After such a haul as you made by the robbery of Blair's £12,000, the comparatively trifling amount which a prudent man like this poor Mr. Shaw would have had about him cannot have had much attraction for either of you. I am sure that robbery was not your object : I want to know what was."

As she took not the least notice of his expressions of indignant astonishment, Meredith suddenly changed his tone, drew forward a chair, and, seating himself in front of her, put his spectacles on his nose and his hands on his knees, and examined her face, with his head tilted back, and a look of genial amusement on his face.

"It's too funny, simply too funny," said he at last, when his effrontery had had its intended effect of making Madeline impatient and restless. " Here's a good lady who has married three gentlemen in succession, without troubling herself about the fact that two of those unions were illegal; then, when she comes across the original and only genuine husband, she thinks herself entitled to bring him to book." He drew his chair a little nearer to her, and continued, wagging his head from side to side as he spoke, in a particularly irritating manner : " Now look here, our days of connubial bliss are over, and so's your right to henpeck me. It isn't likely I'm going to tell tales out of school to please you at this time of day. And if I were to confess to you that I'd murdered "—he shuddered at the word—" half the stockbrokers in Europe, it wouldn't do a bit of good, except to satisfy your idle curiosity, since a wife can't witness against her husband. And you are my wife, Madame de What-you-may-call-'em, and I've only got to open my mouth to have you up for bigamy, so there !"

" But you won't do that : it would take a stronger inducement than that to make you appear in a court of justice in any character."

"All right, all right; perhaps it would. But now, aren't you a silly woman to go poking your nose into things that don't concern you in the least, when the very best thing that can happen to you is to be entirely forgotten by—by certain people in whose affairs you seem determined to meddle? You've heard the proverb 'Let sleeping dogs lie,' and if you had heard certain words which—which certain people made use of in Paris ten years ago, when you turned so unaccountably nasty, I think you would see the advantage of leaving well alone."

"Did you ever hear the words *I* made use of on that occasion?"

"Oh yes, the nonsense a sensible woman will speak in a passion, and be ashamed of when she comes to herself."

This particularly unwise speech made Madeline's cheeks glow and her eyes flash.

"Exactly," she assented, speaking under strong self-restraint. "But, as even a sensible woman may object to see crimes committed with impunity under her very nose, I shall call upon Mr. Beresford, and put him in possession of certain facts in the history of his confidential clerk."

This blow struck home. Meredith jumped up with a deep-drawn breath, and his fist raised in exasperation which, however, was more comical than alarming to Madeline, who only looked up and nodded calmly as an assurance that she was in earnest.

"If you do——" he growled; and he stopped and looked in her face with most careful scrutiny. Then, as if satisfied, he dropped his fist and sat down again.

" You think I don't mean what I say ; but you are mistaken. Or perhaps you fancy that your credit is so good with Mr. Beresford that he will believe nothing against you ? There I think you are mistaken again. Your employer is a selfish, avaricious man, willing to shut his eyes to irregularities on your part which don't concern him and his business. But commercial smartness is not the same thing as robbery preceded by murder ; and if Mr. Beresford were once to understand that you had had a hand in the death of Mr. Shaw——"

"Before God, Madeline, I had not!" burst out the little man, who was by this time shaking from head to foot. "I had nothing to do with it—I know nothing about it. I was shocked. It came upon me like a thunderbolt. Oh, Madeline, you've seen the worst of me!—now, be honest, was I ever cruel?"

He had risen, and was leaning against the rail of the chair he had occupied, bending over it, and speaking with most genuine earnestness and anxiety. Madeline did not look at him, but her mouth quivered. Something in his pleading voice, his momentary sincerity, recalled the old days of their brief married life together, his impulsive remorse after some one of his numerous backslidings, the difficulty she used to feel in assuming for a few minutes that hardness which was now her natural attitude to all the world. She sprang up, walked quickly to one of the two windows, threw it open, and looked out at the masts and funnels of the ships that lined the quay. It was a dark dull night, and the wind was rising. Meredith followed her to

the window, and as she turned suddenly, she
found herself so close to him that she uttered
a hoarse cry. Before she could pass he put
out his hands to detain her, and, shrinking
with disgust from his touch, she stopped.

"Madeline, you must believe this—I will
have you believe this," he said, dropping from
his voice and manner the crust of coarseness
which, at first assumed as an affectation, was
now the result of years of companionship
with his inferiors in education. "There is
only one of the Commandments I've never
broken—I've never helped to break : I've
never lifted up my hand against any man's life.
And there is one oath I've kept and mean to
keep ; and that is to stand by the man who's
stood by me. Not much to take pride in, I
dare say you think. But one creed is as good
as another if you stick to it, and that's mine.
And if you tell on me to old Beresford, you'll
simply lose him a good clerk and take away
from me the one honest occupation I've got,
which I might have settled down to entirely
one of these days. And as for hurting Louis
de Breteuil by this slapdash sort of accusa-

tion, it's like catching a bird by putting salt on its tail. To rush about and proclaim that a certain man is a murderer won't hang him, my dear."

"No ; if it were so easy as that, the excitement wouldn't be strong enough to be worth the trouble."

And the flexible red mouth, so passionate, so changeful in the old days, became straight with the horrible resolution of a sensual nature grown hard and cruel. Meredith absolutely shivered as he looked at her.

"And do you—do—do you mean to—to tell me," he stammered in a low voice, " that you—you would send a man to the gallows *pour passer le temps ?*"

"Not quite that. But the most turbulent life is better than stagnation, and I am not sorry that chance has reminded me of an old grudge to be paid off by throwing me across the path of my creditors."

"One of them. If you were to come across the other you wouldn't get off so well. Look here, Madeline, you'd better get your husband to buy you a couple of new dresses,

and forget all about me and—the other one.
You let us alone, and we'll let you alone. I
don't want any harm to come to you, and I
don't exactly know why, for you're a vin-
dictive devil as ever I've met ; but still, for
the sake of—well, I don't exactly know what,
for we never were very comfortable together,
and no wonder, considering how you've
turned out. Still, there's a spirit in you I
like, and what I say to you is : Humbug
about here if you like ; go and worry old
Beresford, try to set my employers against me,
if you like—remember I've got the ear of
both the money-grubbing old boys—but for
God's sake don't try to meet De Breteuil.
I'm only a human blackguard, but he is—the
devil."

And Meredith took up from the table the
shabby, low-crowned, curly-brimmed round
hat which was his habitual and most unbe-
coming headgear, nodded to Madeline in
exactly the same awkward would-be careless
manner with which, during their married life
together, he used to leave her to go out in
the evening " to see a man who'd got a tip,"

and opened the door. Half-way along the corridor he met a tall gentleman with a gray moustache, who stared at him, but in a manner too dignified to be called impertinent. Mr. Smith touched his hat to him, and hurried along, wondering how Madeline would explain his own visit. "Old chap worships her, I suppose; and he might be at the bottom of the sea for what she cares; so might I. But De Breteuil—I'll be hanged if I know whether she isn't fond of him still. Queer creatures, women." These reflections lasted till he reached the platform, where he found that his train had gone; however, he started for Boulogne by the next, and it was some weeks before Mr. Smith again made his appearance in Calais or its neighbourhood.

The ten days following the night of Mr. Shaw's murder were spent in investigation by the police, in arresting and releasing various persons who had no connection with the affair, and in interrogating all those people who had had any intercourse whatever with Mr. Shaw on the day of his death. Gerald, Mr. Beresford, and Mr. Smith were the only

people who could tell anything of importance;
but the first was ill of concussion of the brain,
the last had disappeared with the telegraphic
excuse to his employers that urgent family
affairs required his presence in England ; so
that Mr. Beresford's sensational announcement that the dead man had had in his
possession a clue to the perpetrators of the
robbery in the train was the only important
piece of evidence forthcoming.   Mr. Shaw's
eldest son, a goodhearted young fellow, with
the manners of a groom, who had been most
carefully educated without learning anything
at all, came over to Calais, to call at " Les
Bouleaux " to see Mr. Beresford and to take
his father's body back to England when the
inquest was over.   He behaved very well,
poor perplexed young man, looking dignified
for the first time in his life as he stood, in his
long travelling ulster, silenced by his grief
and by his ignorance of the French language,
listening by the hour to explanations and
declarations by first one official and then
another, none of whom could tell him more
than he knew—that his father had been foully

murdered, no one knew by whom. So he left a kind, indifferently spelt letter at the house of M. Fournier, to be given to Gerald as soon as he was better, and returned with his solemn freight to England. And there were more investigations, and more interrogatories, and at the end of a fortnight Gerald, having sufficiently recovered from his illness, had his evidence taken down and his careful description of the murderer. On being asked whether the face was like anyone he had seen before, the young man at first hesitated, but finally said " No," and persisted in that answer.

But when, a fortnight after the murder, Madame de Lancry called to learn how he was, and, finding him convalescent, broached the subject of that night's adventures, he was more communicative, and on her pressing him to be frank with her, he confessed that the face he had seen bending over him in the darkness had struck him by its likeness to Victor Fournier.

" It was only a likeness in the features, you understand, madame, and I think he was a much older man than Victor : but he had just the same type of thin aquiline features, and a small black moustache like Victor's."

Madame de Lancry looked at him, and listened attentively.

" Had you ever seen the man before ?" she asked.

" Never, madame."

" Ah !" She got up and walked about the room, looking at the objects around her, glancing now and then at Gerald, whose languid interest in the matter under discussion, though scarcely surprising so soon after his illness, irritated and astonished her. At last she stopped in front of him, such a majestic figure in her trained gown of black brocade glistening with hanging drops of jet, that the pause she made before speaking rendered her slow, grave words doubly impressive.

" What would you say," she asked solemnly, " if I were to tell you that the object you hold dearest in life is intimately connected with the discovery of Mr. Shaw's murderer ?"

Gerald started, and his face grew very white.

" Why, what has she to do with it ?" he faltered quickly, in a husky voice.

" She !" said Madame de Lancry, in a deep voice that sounded like distant thunder to the poor lad, who grew suddenly as red as he had been white, and hung his head, and fidgeted with the tassel of the sofa-cushion like a corrected child.

"I mean—I mean," said he, clearing his throat, " that I do not understand you, madame."

" You told me, not three weeks ago—but you very young men measure your constancy, your convictions, by minutes, I know," she interpolated scornfully—" that the one object of your life was to clear your father's name from the suspicion which still hangs over it."

Gerald started again. " Yes, yes, so it is," he said quickly, his thin face burning and quivering with half a dozen strong and strange emotions as he heard her.

Madame de Lancry watched the sensitive

and ingenuous face steadily, and said, in a low deep voice, the very tone of which kept him spell-bound : " Find the murderer of Mr. Shaw—and you will have found the man who robbed and murdered your father."

The shock of this declaration, made to him while he was still weak from illness, was too much for Gerald. He looked up in her face quite steadily for a moment longer, and then his body fell forward, and he was only pre-vented by the quick clasp of her strong arms from falling to the floor. Her first impulse, even then, was indignant contempt at the weakness of a nature which was not braced up instead of shaken by a statement so over-whelming. But as she put her arm round the young man's shoulder, and laid his damp head back gently on to the cushions of the sofa, the old emotion of tenderness, which she had not now known for years, woke up in the woman's breast again, and she re-membered the time when thoughts of love were foremost in her too.

" Poor boy !" she whispered kindly ; and as she touched his hair with her lips with motherly gentleness the door opened, and Victor came in.

He had just returned home from the factory, and, on hearing that Madame de Lancry was in the *salon*, he had hurried to the room in eager haste, for his admiration for this somewhat inaccessible lady was increasing every day. Of course he affected not even to have seen her caressing attitude near Gerald, although she scarcely altered it on his entrance; but when she left, after a few remarks to Victor, in which she did not forget to congratulate him on his approaching marriage, the young Frenchman turned almost savagely to Gerald, and said disagreeably:

"She might have spared a little of her sympathy for me, linked as I shall be to-morrow to the most ill-tempered specimen of boldness and prudery your fog-smothered country has ever produced!"

Gerald looked hurt and angry, but he only said, after a pause, "To-morrow?"

"Yes, to-morrow. Old Beresford is going to give a confounded betrothal-dinner, to tie us up by anticipation, you know; he has grown very solicitous since my aunt's death the other day."

This was an allusion to the fact that a rich widowed sister of M. Fournier's, a lady who had been for some years in delicate health, had died within the last week in the south of France, leaving the bulk of her property to her nephew Victor.

Gerald listened, but made no answer; and when, some few minutes later, Victor, not finding him a lively companion, left him alone, he remained for some time in the attitude he had assumed on first hearing the news, leaning forward with his elbows on his knees and his hands clasped loosely together. Presently he got up with red eyes and tremulous lips, and walking unsteadily towards the mantelpiece, saw that it was three o'clock.

" There's lots of time for me to get there before they have dinner," he said to himself; " and of course I really ought to make some inquiries and bestir myself, after what Madame de Lancry said."

So he went in search of Madame Fournier,

told her with tears of gratitude for her kindness in his eyes that he must go back to "Les Bouleaux" that day, and show Mr. Beresford that he was fit for work again—which he evidently was not—and started in a small hired omnibus within half an hour of making up his mind.

The drive was full of horrible reminiscences to him, but as he drew near to "Les Bouleaux" his agitation increased from another cause. Suddenly, within a few yards of the entrance to the avenue, he shouted to the driver to stop, and got out of the omnibus. For he had caught sight of a little dark figure that started forward out of the open gate to meet him.

CHAPTER VII.

On seeing Peggy waiting for him at the white gate of the avenue, Gerald checked the impulse which had made him run a few steps towards her, and deliberately paid and dismissed the driver of the omnibus before he even looked at her again. Then he raised his hat and walked slowly and rather stiffly towards where she was standing. He felt very nervous, and grew alternately hot and cold as he came near her; but in spite of the agitation which made him for the first time shy in her presence, he could not help thinking what a very odd welcome she was giving him.

For, instead of returning the smile his face wore as he advanced, she stood looking at him gravely and as he thought coldly until

he was within a few paces ; then he held out
his hand, and with one fierce little stare she
quickly threw her arms behind her and
clasped her fingers tightly together behind
her back. Gerald stopped, utterly disconcerted.

" Miss Beresford !" he stammered.

But this brought on the climax. She
turned her back upon him abruptly, and
marched down the avenue towards the house
as fast as her small feet could with proper
dignity carry her. For a moment he stood
where she had left him, too much bewildered
to follow ; then he ran after her, and, keeping
by her side as she walked on without taking
the least notice of his presence except to turn
her head the other way, he pleaded for an explanation with all his shyness dissolved in
consternation.

" Miss Beresford ! Miss Beresford !
What *is* the matter ? What have I done ?
Why do you treat me like this ? Won't you
speak to me ? Peggy ! for goodness' sake
don't go on like this ! Didn't you want me
ever to come back, didn't you ?" he panted,

growing rather exhausted in these combined mental and physical efforts.

But still she took not the slightest notice of him. So he gathered himself together for one last appeal, and said, catching his breath:

" Well, I—I can't run after you any more, because I've just been ill ; but it's very unkind of you, and I thought you had more heart."

She stopped short and turned upon him fiercely, and he saw to his great astonishment that she was actually shaking with rage.

" Unkind ! You call me unkind ! When I've been lying awake every night thinking about you, and walking up and down this avenue all day long whenever I could get away from them, because I didn't dare to ask when you were coming back, and I—I hoped, I—I always hoped to see you coming ; and then at last when you do come, you—you pretend not to see me, and—and—you have a long conversation with the omnibus driver —I saw you—I saw you—and then walk up to me as stiffly and coldly as if I were a chance acquaintance. And when I'm just going to be married to that hateful Victor, too! Oh, it is you who are unkind!"

And she laid her head down on the black palings that ran along the right side of the avenue, and sobbed. After a few minutes, however, as Gerald did not attempt to comfort her, as she had expected, she raised her head to look at him. The expression of his face made her leave off crying; but a mere look of pain in a man's eyes won't satisfy the least exacting of women, and she said in a querulous voice, as she dried her eyes : " You might say something nice to me, Gerald, when I'm so miserable, and all about you."

" I—I don't know what to say to you," stammered he, in a strangled voice, looking over her head.

" Well, say you're glad to see me," said she, coming a step nearer to him and glancing up most piteously.

" Of course I'm not glad to see you when you're miserable," he answered impatiently.

" Well, but I can't dance and sing and laugh when I'm unhappy."

"Then I don't want to see you till you are happy again."

"That means that you never want to see me again, then, for I shall be miserable for the rest of my life."

Then Gerald looked down at her, for her tone of childish complaint had changed to that of a woman's despair. He was surprised and shocked to see how old her face had suddenly become. She was no longer petulant, she was hopeless. In this mood, however, he could trust himself to talk to her.

"What do you mean?" he asked, in a voice that was not quite steady.

"I—I don't think I ought to trouble you by telling you," said she, with sudden reticence. "We will talk about it by-and-by, another time, when you are quite well. Now I think we had better go in, hadn't we? For it can't be long before dinner-time."

Gerald assented, and they walked on together rather awkwardly. The young girl seemed shy and ashamed of herself, and she talked very fast about trifling matters, scarcely waiting for the short answers he was able to give her. As they stepped inside the hall her manner suddenly changed again, and she said in a low and broken voice, hanging her head :

" I am sorry I was so impatient and rude. But since that night—you know "—and they both shivered—" this house has been worse than haunted. I've become hysterical, foolish, idiotic. You'll forgive me, won't you ?"

She did not hold out her hand with her natural frank and impulsive coquetry ; she kept her eyes on the tiled floor and played with the buttons of her ulster. Gerald looked down at her black velvet hat. She heard him breathing heavily, and the next moment she heard his voice close to her ear.

" Yes, I forgive you, I'd forgive you anything. But—it kills me to see you unhappy," he whispered gruffly ; " I can't bear it ; I'd jump into the sea to make you lively and bright again—you know I would, you *must* know."

She looked up. But no sooner had his last words fallen from his lips than he turned away from her, and slunk off quickly towards the staircase. She made one step to follow him, and stopped as the *salon* door opened.

" Who's that ?" asked Miss M'Leod's thin little voice ; " surely I heard Gerald's step."

" Yes, he's come ; he's just gone up-stairs," said Peggy quietly ; and she followed the housekeeper, who overflowed with voluble comments on the unceremonious manner of his reappearance among them, up the stair-case to dress for dinner.

Gerald had reached his room in such a dis-turbed state of mind that for a few minutes he could only march up and down the narrow promenade between his bed and the heavy wardrobe which took up the greater part of the rest of the apartment, without any more distinct idea in his head than that he was suffering horribly. But when he reached the door for about the tenth time he stopped short, and bent his head to listen to the sound of women's footsteps coming up the stairs. The precise trot-trot of the pair of feet that reached the landing first had no particular effect on him, though their owner, Miss

M'Leod, had been his staunch friend ever since his coming to " Les Bouleaux." But those lighter, slower, lazier steps that followed, dragging wearily over the waxed uncarpeted corridor, seemed to fall one by one on his own heart as he leaned against the door, with the hot glow of passion on his face, and his damp hand fixed firmly on the handle, that no slightest vibration of the old boards should deaden for one moment the light footfall that was music to him. He stood there in the ecstasy of a young man's first passion, not in the least understanding how it was that his short, feverish, unsatisfactory interview of ten minutes ago with Peggy had ripened what had been the haunting fancy of his illness into a fiery yearning which made him kiss the very wall which lay nearest to her room, although Miss M'Leod's apartment, presumably a non-conductor of the love-current, interposed between the chamber where the young madman was now frantically cuddling a withered sprig of palm-blossom which he had regarded with comparatively calm interest at the time his darling had given it to him a fortnight ago, and the room where Peggy herself, in a fit of despair at the position of human affairs, was lying face downwards on the bed, and wishing that stupid, unresponsive Gerald had remained in Calais.

For all the woman was not awake in her yet, and she did not quite know why she had been so anxious for Gerald's return, and so disappointed at the manner of it. And she went downstairs to dinner feeling sulky and ill-used, and would have been quite rude in her coldness to Gerald if he had not studiously abstained from so much as looking at her, and confined his attention throughout dinner entirely to his employer and Miss M'Leod.

The young clerk's return was such a welcome relief to the gloom into which Mr. Shaw's tragic death had plunged the entire household, that everybody in the house made some sort of attempt to celebrate his return, from Mr. Beresford, who broke through his usual parsimony so far as to replace the daily *vin ordinaire* by a bottle of inferior St. Julien,

down to Henri the coachman, who blacked
all M. Gérald's boots and shoes, polished
them into an unaccustomed brightness, and
placed them in an imposing row along the
wall outside the young gentleman's door.
The flattering nature of this action was due
to the fact that it had never been properly
decided whether the blacking was Pierre's or
Henri's work, and, to avoid conflicts, Gerald
more often than not did the work himself.

Gerald's bold policy of ignoring the girl
who had set his heart on fire answered admir-
ably as long as dinner lasted. Miss M'Leod
always presided at the table, owing to Mr.
Beresford's infirmity. The master of the
house sat at her left hand, and had that side
of the table all to himself, so that Pierre
could minister to his wants quite unimpeded.
Opposite to him were the chairs of his
daughter and the young clerk, the latter being
nearest to Miss M'Leod.

On this occasion Gerald did not absolutely
neglect his small neighbour, for he passed her
the mustard, and saved her from a blow with
a plate which Delphine, who had not yet

overcome a rough-and-ready manner of waiting at table, was on the point of accidentally
administering; but he did not address one
word to her, and she revenged herself by refusing to laugh at small jokes of his which
Miss M'Leod received quite hilariously, and
by staring in moody and hostile silence at the
green shade over her father's eyes, without
showing the least interest in an account of
the reported discovery of gold mines in Sicily,
which Gerald had read about in the morning
papers, and to which the avaricious old paralytic listened with avidity.

But when they all adjourned to the inner
salon, and Mr. Beresford, refusing the offer of
himself as an opponent, which Gerald
hastened to make, sat down to chess with
Miss M'Leod—to whom he had to give four
to six pieces, beating her easily again and
again under those conditions — Gerald's
brilliancy suddenly evaporated on finding
himself thus left to entertain the remaining
lady. Having placed her favourite chair by
the fire for her in her favourite position, and
received in acknowledgment the coldest,

most perfunctory of "Thank you's," he sat down opposite to her, took up the last number of the *Graphic*, which Mr. Beresford received weekly from England, and asked, in a voice of such well-acted indifference that it sounded absolutely uncivil, whether she had finished reading it.

"Yes, thank you," said she, in a tremulous voice, looking at him at last, with eyes so expressive of surprise and pain at his curtness that Gerald fancied the instinctive movement he made towards her must have attracted the attention of everyone in the room.

He glanced at the pair at the chessboard.

Miss M'Leod had chirped out "Check," making the slight mistake of taking a bishop for her queen. Mr. Beresford, who had to play with his left hand, had taken the erring bishop with a knight, chuckling as he did so. The opponents were now rejoicing together over this feat, for the devoted little housekeeper was always good-humouredly pleased when her own imbecile play afforded her employer a minute's cheap satisfaction.

Gerald glanced back from the elderly pair intent on their game to the face of the girl sitting opposite to him ; he could only see a very little of it, just the outline of her cheek as she looked away from him, intent apparently on a book which was lying open on her lap. He was growing very hot, very miserable, and he turned over the leaves of the *Graphic* with staring eyes which criticised the pictures carefully, and read the words underneath them, but without taking in their meaning. No attempt at concentrating his attention could blind him to the fact that Peggy never turned a page, and presently he heard a faint sound that deadened his senses to everything else ; it was the fall of a tear on to the book on her knee.

Now, this new love of his he had already recognised as a temptation which must be wrestled with, subdued, and then ignored if possible : for to cherish it, and, as it were, take it out from time to time to be looked at, was, he knew, quite incompatible with keeping it a profound secret from the girl who had inspired it. This resolution was an excellent one, and, if it had not been for that tear, it might have stood firm at least until the following morning ; but as it was, the voluptuous anguish of watching the poor little lady whom he would fain have been comforting, as her small fingers stole to her pocket, drew out her handkerchief, and passed it furtively across her eyes, was an indulgence not to be resisted ; and so it came to pass that when Peggy gave a hasty glance round her to assure herself that her outbreak had not been noticed, her eyes met Gerald's and read in them a most eloquent message. She turned away her head again with a blush, but she could not lose the consciousness of his gaze, and after a few seconds she rose quickly and left the room.

Gerald could hear her steps on the polished floor of the outer *salon*, and after one vain attempt to compose himself to reading, he let his paper drop on to the floor, and stole quietly into the next room. There was a lamp there on one of the side-tables, and he saw that Peggy had pulled aside the blind, and was looking out of the long French window.

She heard him coming, but she did not turn round.

" What were you crying for?" he whispered very gently.

" I wasn't crying."

This was a *cul-de-sac.* Gerald went back and tried another opening.

" Are there many people coming to-morrow ?"

" Yes, I believe so. Priests and Levites and all the necessary functionaries."

" You mean—that it is a sacrifice—this engagement ?" said he, with hesitation, after a pause.

" Of course it is. Poor Victor !"

" But, Peggy, you know—you know the dinner to-morrow doesn't bind you to any-thing ; it doesn't oblige you to marry a man you really dislike."

To Gerald's discomfiture, this kindly-meant suggestion brought down upon him an avalanche of wrath.

" I dislike !" she echoed, turning upon him in amazement much more haughty than if she had been an empress. " I don't understand you, Mr. Staunton. Do you think I should have accepted M. Fournier if I had not loved him ?"

For a moment Gerald was overwhelmed. But her wild and inconsistent behaviour irritated him so much in his excitable and feverish mood, that he at last exclaimed with sudden passion :

"I'm sorry I misunderstood you. I might have expected that you would express your love, as you do your other feelings, in some eccentric manner."

He was torn with remorse the next moment ; for without looking at him, without answering him, she thrust down her head into her little hands, and, with one long sob that seemed to vibrate in his own heart, she ran quickly past him and out of the room.

He was ready to dash his head against the wall by this time, and after a futile rush in pursuit of her, hearing the housekeeper's piping voice calling to know what the floor-scraping and door-slamming was about, he escaped into the garden.

The young fellow had no suspicion of the

reason for Peggy's strange conduct, and it would have been very hard to make him believe that the feeling which prompted her to be rude and fierce and disagreeable was but a stage of the same infatuation which caused his own hands to tremble when he came near her, and his face to glow with illogical adoration when the precious opportunity arrived of watching her unobserved. But the strongest impression her extravagant behaviour left upon him, as he marched up and down the sandy paths under the poplar and birch trees, was that she was unhappy, and that he had been most selfishly impatient with her.

" Poor little thing ! poor little thing !" he murmured to himself, as he drew near the swing and pulled the cord gently backwards and forwards, in tender memory of their morning's amusement there a fortnight ago. " She doesn't care for Victor, whatever she may say—and what is more, I don't believe she ever will. At least I'm afraid—— If I were only rich ! If I only had the brains to make myself rich some day ! If I could only think— God! what's the good of thinking, when it all can only end one way? I must go grinding on at my thirty shillings a week, and think myself lucky to get that, while she is married away to a man she doesn't care about, just because he can give her a lot of handsome dresses that she doesn't want. And all the while I believe she would be as happy as a bird in a cottage out there on the sand-dunes, with—with anybody who would pet her and love her as— Oh, well, it's no good thinking about it!"

And with much effort and some shame, he turned his thoughts to the strange revelation made to him that afternoon by Madame de Lancry. She had given him no proof of her strange assertion that his father and Mr. Shaw had been murdered by the same man, no slightest clue to help him in tracking the man down. The shock of her words had been so great as to render him incapable at the time of framing any question as to the course he ought to pursue, and after some thought he decided that the first step to take was to see little Jules, and question him as to what he

had seen on the night when he had been
pulled out screaming and struggling from
under the dead bushes and grasses of the
wood near "Les Bouleaux."

"He took me for Monnier," Gerald re-
flected, "and he had evidently seen something which Monnier did not wish him to see.
The old rascal is mixed up somehow with
this awful business, I know. Perhaps this
little urchin can put me on the scent. I
wish I had questioned him the very next
day."

The mistake he had made in not doing so
was soon apparent; for on arriving at the
miserable little two-roomed cabin which *la
mère* Benoit had shared with her grandson and
some remarkably long-legged and unproduc-
tive fowls, he found it tenantless. He struck
a match and examined both the damp
draughty rooms: they looked scarcely more
bare and comfortless than before. In one,
the ashes of a small fire were still on the
hearth; in both, the miserable furniture, not
worth the trouble of carrying away, remained
to prove the independence of the very poor.

There was just enough dust, just enough disorder in the wretched wreck of a home to show that the thrifty old woman had left it never to return; and Gerald walked out into the open air again with a foreboding that this departure was Monnier's work, and that the reason must be a grave one.

After a few minutes' thought he walked in the direction of the gamekeeper's dwelling. That the man himself would be impenetrable he knew; but if Babette should chance to be in a good humour, he might learn something from her. She generally spent the evenings of the colder months knitting quietly in the cottage in the company of her grandmother, an insipid, silent, and prematurely aged woman who counted for little in the household: her father was usually away, in more lively society, at the *cabaret.* Gerald did not hope much from this visit, and his first peep into the cottage, when Madame Monnier herself opened the door, did not tend to encourage him.

For the gamekeeper was smoking by the fire, and Babette was not there.

CHAPTER VIII.

A CRY broke from old Madame Monnier's lips as Gerald entered the gamekeeper's cottage. She was silenced by two words from her surly son, who, in his seat by the fire, just pulled off his cap and took his pipe for a moment from his mouth in ungracious welcome, while the old woman brought forward a chair for the young gentleman, still staring at him with vacant mistrust.

"What's the matter, granny?" said he, putting his hand gently on her arm. Madame Monnier, who, by the way, looked scarcely older or more weatherbeaten than her son, was not reputed to be overburdened with wits; and the feeble friendliness she usually showed to Gerald was considered an unflattering preference.

This evening, however, something had evidently happened to trouble her weak wits, for she drew herself away from his touch, mumbling incoherently and in a low voice.

"Don't mind her," said the gamekeeper sharply; and he signed to her that her presence was no longer wanted, with an extra wrinkle in his ugly face which caused her to shuffle hastily into the next room.

"What's your business, monsieur?" he then asked.

But that was the very last thing that Gerald would have thought of disclosing to him. So he said he wanted to hear whether *la mère's* rheumatism was better, and what had become of Babette. At this mention of the girl's name the gamekeeper's little eyes fastened on him; but the subject had lost much of its interest to Gerald lately, and although he grew red under Monnier's keen glance, he was not much disconcerted by it.

"My mother's rheumatism is no better; she can't expect it at her age. And Babette —why, she's gone away—to service."

" To service!" repeated Gerald, in astonishment.

" Yes ; why not ? I don't approve of keeping a great strapping girl idle at home, to have her head turned by some philandering fool, while her old father is out toiling to keep her in luxury."

" Oh !" said Gerald quite simply. The gamekeeper's speech had ignored all the facts of the case so completely that assent and dissent were alike out of the question. He wondered whether he himself was the " philandering fool " alluded to, or whether the term was meant for the stranger he had seen with Babette. And then his vague fear grew stronger that the girl was in some way linked with the man about whom he had such grave suspicions ; and Gerald, who had no skill in hiding his feelings, found himself returning the gamekeeper's sidelong looks with a wide stare of open mistrust. As soon as he became conscious of this the young fellow started up, hot and uncomfortable ; he knew that he had failed as a detective, so he threw off the character.

" Look here, Monnier," said he, leaning against the high stone chimneypiece and uneasily kicking one of the burning logs, with his eyes fixed on the fire, " I wish you would tell me where she's gone. I don't want to go after her, you needn't think that—Babette and I were always great chums, you know, and of course we're not children now ; but I can't help feeling a great interest in her, and—and I should really be awfully glad to know that she—that she is all right, in fact."

" *Sacre-re-re*, monsieur!" growled the gamekeeper, " I should think if her father is satisfied as to her safety, that is enough. And it is very good of you to interest yourself about her, but she is in better hands than— yours." And he looked straight at Gerald with mean and impudent suspicion in every line of his face.

The young man grew red, with alarm as well as anger. He thrust his hands into his pockets and faced the older man steadily.

" Well, I can't make you speak," said he after a minute's pause. " But I know some-

body who can. You know very well it's
nonsense to pretend you suspect my motives,
because you don't. I never had a motive in
my life that wasn't clean compared to the
best of yours. For you've something more
to account for than Babette's going away. I
saw you sneaking along the road from Calais
on the night of the murder, and it's my belief
you know something about it, you infernal
old fox !"

Gerald had meant to keep this suspicion a
dead secret ; but the sight of the gamekeeper,
doubled up as if to keep not only his mind
but his person as much to himself as possible,
blinking and squinting at him cautiously in
the firelight, so irritated the young man that
he blurted out the accusing words almost
against his own will.

Monnier stuck out his lean pointed chin,
pursed up his blue lips, and blinked at his
visitor more persistently than ever, but without giving any intimation that his sensitive
nature was wounded. Gerald's hands twitched
in his pockets during a rather awkward
silence. Then the injured one nodded his

head slowly two or three times with a cackling laugh of generous contempt.

"It's very easy to come here," he began mockingly, "and to say hard words to a poor old man when you find that his daughter is no longer about to say soft ones to. And you young gentlemen think poor men were only made for you to kick, and poor women for you to kiss." Gerald looked as if on the point of illustrating part of this theory. "But there is a heaven above, monsieur——"

"Yes, and there's something else underneath," interrupted Gerald hotly, "and you'll get what you deserve some day, if you don't now."

"The saints watch over the innocent, monsieur," said the gamekeeper with grotesque resignation, "and you and your flaunting madam won't get much out of your spying visits here."

Gerald looked at him puzzled. Had Madame de Lancry been here already? And had she failed, as entirely as he himself had done, in extracting anything worth hearing from the leather-skinned old rascal? The

bewilderment on his face encouraged Monnier,
who went on in a much more assured tone :
" I should like to know what your patron
Mr. Beresford would say, if I was to go
and complain of your hanging about here
after my girl ? Why, it would be enough to
get you turned out of his house, that it
would."

His righteous indignation carried him just
a little too far. Gerald, though simple
enough to be deceived by the blue-eyed young
girl, had seen through the craft of her less
fascinating father. So he said quietly :
" You've changed your tune very suddenly,
Monnier, after thanking me so warmly as you
did six weeks ago for my kindness to your
old mother and Babette. As you've grown
so suspicious, I'd better give you a chance of
making a proper complaint to Mr. Beresford."

For the first time the man was disconcerted.
His withered skin took a bluish tint, and his
knotty hands clutched the wooden sides of
his chair.

" Come, M. Gérald," said he after a few

moments' pause, with a futile effort to be genial, " old friends like you and me don't quarrel except in fun. I get lonely and fretful now o' nights—I miss my daughter," he went on, ignoring the fact that when Babette was at home he always spent his evenings at the *cabaret*. " Far be it from me to say a word that could harm you to M. Beresford. It was all a boy and girl friendship between you and Babette, I know ; though perhaps the old patron, being so austere, might not see how innocent it was."

From under his shaggy eyebrows he watched Gerald, who, however, gave no sign of being intimidated by this suggestion.

"I think he will see the matter in the right light, Monnier," he said steadily ; " at any rate, I'll take my chance of that."

Turning quickly, with a strong sense of having had enough of the gamekeeper's society, the young man was already at the door, when he felt the grip of a sinewy hand upon his arm. Monnier's face was puckered up into ugly wrinkles of fear and anxiety as he detained his guest.

" You wouldn't say anything to get a poor
old man into trouble, would you?" said he,
with a most unattractive whine of blustering
entreaty. "I've been a good servant to M.
Beresford, but a word from a young gentleman so high in his confidence as monsieur
might do me harm, which I'm sure I've
never deserved. And on mere suspicion, and
such childish suspicion too! Monsieur would
surely never harm a poor old man——"

Gerald tore himself away, opened the door,
and let himself out, without one more glance
at the blinking foxy eyes that watched him
furtively in the darkness as he dashed down
the narrow red-tiled garden-path and out
at the gate. As he turned into the road,
on his way back to "Les Bouleaux," he
thought he heard a weak voice quavering
out his name : " M. Gérald." But he
paid no attention to the faint cry, almost
believing it to be the work of his fancy, until
he heard the cottage-door slammed by the
irritated gamekeeper, and immediately after
the footsteps of a woman on the road behind
him. He stopped, looked round, and found

himself face to face with old Madame Monnier. Her manner was more wavering and witless than ever, but she was in such piteous distress that Gerald's heart was touched, and he submitted to be clawed by her thin fingers and to be treated to a long pointless discourse, in which she alternately reviled him for " taking her granddaughter away " and implored him to " get her back from the wolf."

" It's all right, *la mère ;* the wolf won't do Babette any harm," said he soothingly.

He had no hope of learning anything from the old woman's incoherent wailings, and he was startled when, after staring blankly into his face for a few moments without speaking, she croaked out : " And they say Paris is such a wicked place ! Oh, I have heard such tales of what becomes of poor country girls when they get there !"

" Paris !" said Gerald, with suddenly vivid interest. " Has Babette gone to Paris, do you say ?"

His vehemence frightened her, and it was some minutes before he could get her to con-

fess that " ce beau monsieur " had said she
would be quite safe there, and that she would
be rich and happy and a great lady.

At this confirmation of his worst fears con-
cerning his old playfellow, Gerald turned
upon the old woman so savagely that she
broke away from him and tottered back to
the gate of the cottage. He followed her
halfway up the garden-path, but as she
glanced in terror at the door, and gave him
no answer to his questions but disconnected
mumblings, he turned back impatiently, and
took a short cut to " Les Bouleaux," with
his mind full of new anxiety. Everyone had
gone to bed, but as he crept softly upstairs to
his room, and paused a moment at the top of
the stairs, he fancied he heard a faint sound
of sobbing from Peggy's room. A throb of
tenderness in the young man's heart was succeeded by an impulse of rage against the man
who was to be her husband.

" To give a girl like that to a fellow that
doesn't care for her ! How can Mr. Beresford have the heart to do it ?" he thought to
himself bitterly, as he stole to his own room,

not for wholesome sleep, but for untimely
consideration of the hopeless muddle into
which human affairs seemed to have got.
After passing most of the night in reflections
which he considered philosophical, while they
were only love-sick, he of course came downstairs on the following morning in the seediest
and sorriest of moods. He was glad Peggy
had not yet appeared; he gobbled up his
breakfast in a great hurry to be off to the
office, and was furious when Mr. Beresford,
in the fulness of his heart, sent down Pierre
to say that, as to-day was to be a fête
in honour of his daughter's engagement,
M. Gérald would please return from the
office in time to receive M. Beresford's
guests.

Gerald's face fell as he drove off to St.
Pierre. A ghastly tribe they would be, these
relations of the Fourniers, appalling in their
monotonous scandalmongering respectability.
However, there was nothing for it but to
submit; so at half-past two the unlucky
young clerk returned to "Les Bouleaux,"
and a little later he was seated in the outer

salon, among antique spinster cousins, high-dried and dull uncles and aunts, two or three plump and effusive young girls of the boisterously ingenuous sort, a couple of particularly offensive spoilt children, and the Fourniers themselves.

Mr. Beresford had retired to the inner *salon* with a chosen pair of prosy old gentlemen whom he left to entertain each other; his feeble health was sufficient excuse for his withdrawal from the clamour in the next room, where poor Peggy had to undergo a martyrdom in the midst of a group of ladies who pulled her about like a doll, and asked her questions suited to the intelligence of a child of six, and found the unhappy little foreigner very amusing. At last her patience gave way, when a well-meaning sister of Madame Fournier's asked her indulgently whether she was not enchanted to find her appointed husband so good-looking and charming.

"No, madame," answered Peggy with simple savagery, while her cheeks flushed and her eyes blazed. "A handsome husband admires himself and charms other women; and nobody who pleases my father could possibly please me."

To the intense relief of Gerald, who overheard this appalling speech in the corner where he was trying to restrain the naughtiest of the spoilt children from hacking off the knobs of a carved armchair with his penknife, the ladies received it as a great joke and repeated it to Victor; and the young clerk was unutterably thankful when half-past five struck, and they all sat down to dinner in the *salle*, and something even more interesting than a half-civilized bride at last drew their attention from the unhappy Peggy.

The room was not very large, every corner was quickly occupied; Peggy jerked her own chair violently into that of her right-hand neighbour, and made room for Gerald on her left.

"Come and sit by me, Gerald," she whispered eagerly, under cover of the clatter and rustle of the general movement, "and then I needn't see so much of that smirking chattering Frenchman." And she glanced at

28—2

Victor, who was charming the staid community of relations by his vivacity, and collecting materials for a burlesque of the whole entertainment by-and-by.

Gerald sat down by her side, but he would not talk to her. Her little sad, bewildered face, as she sat silently amidst the babble, moved him so much that he could scarcely trust himself to look in her direction. He was growing miserable and moonstruck, when some words spoken at the other end of the table roused his attention.

"And how is it Mr. Smith is not here to-day?" old M. Fournier was asking.

"Oh, he couldn't get back here in time," answered Mr. Beresford.

"I can't think what keeps him in London," the other went on. "Smith's erratic manner of doing business I never can understand."

"But the business gets done," broke in Mr. Beresford quickly.

"Yes, yes. And if you are satisfied, I ought to be. Still, I can't help thinking our friend has been growing more erratic and independent than ever lately, and what there is to detain him in London at this time of year I can't imagine. When there's work calling him to Paris, too!"

"Ah, I hope your firm has a hand in the furnishing of M. de Breteuil's new house at St. Cloud!" broke in a stout and pompous brother-in-law, with a round head, close-cropped black hair, and a much-waxed moustache and imperial. "A perfect palace I believe it is to be."

Gerald grew hot, remembering suddenly Mr. Shaw's words about the confidential clerk's underhand dealings with this rich client of Mr. Beresford.

"Yes, yes, we had a large order from him some time ago."

"Ah, if all noblemen had as much money as he, and spent it as freely, we men of commerce should not be such good Republicans, should we?" continued the pompous brother-in-law. "I saw him in the Champs Elysées yesterday, and at the Opéra one day last week; and each time I said to myself, as I looked at him, 'There is something in old blood after all; he might be a prince, that

man !' With his tall figure, as slim and as
straight as that of my nephew Victor there,
and—why, yes, a face not unlike Victor's
either, only a little older, a little thinner :
more interesting, I suppose the ladies would
say."

Gerald shivered. This description recalled
the face that had glared into his in the darkness on the night of the murder, and he was
glad that the talk was turned into another
channel by the interruption of another tactless old gentleman.

" Well, I don't think Victor need complain,
when within ten days he has come into a
fortune and gained a charming girl for a
wife."

" I can't imagine how it was that Mademoiselle Ernestine hit upon Victor to leave
her money to, when she had never seen him,
and could scarcely even have heard his name,
living down in the south as she did."

Mr. Beresford's luck in having settled upon
his daughter quite a modest *dot* just two days
before his future son-in-law became the unexpected possessor of a large fortune had been

the subject of much envious comment. A clue to the mystery appeared suddenly from a most unexpected quarter.

"Oh, but you forget that Mr. Beresford has been spending his winter down there," began Miss M'Leod innocently, when a slight, quick movement of the paralytic's head made her stop short, with the blood rushing to her cheeks.

But it was too late. A roar of ironical laughter showed that in the innocence of her heart the poor little housekeeper had betrayed her scheming master; and though the universal respect for Mr. Beresford, which this discovery of his successful cunning only increased, caused the merriment to be quickly suppressed, the whole story came out after dinner, when the ladies surrounded Miss M'Leod, and forced her unwillingly to acknowledge that Mademoiselle Ernestine had been at Nice while Mr. Beresford was there, that they had often met, and that the name of Victor, with mention of his courage, industry, piety, and other good qualities, might have cropped up now and then in conversation.

Miss M'Leod, who was too honest to deny what she knew to be facts, was, however, certain that no interested thought had suggested to her master this high praise of his partner's son.

She was trying to think of an excuse for escaping from the throng of laughing ladies, and was yet in doubt what reception she might meet from Mr. Beresford, who had retired again to the inner *salon*, when the door was flung roughly open by Delphine, who ushered in, without announcement, a lady whose appearance, unknown as she was, cast all the chattering group into silence.

Tall, beautiful, majestic, she advanced into the room like a queen, her heavily jetted black silk train making subdued music as she moved.

"Madame de Lancry!" cried Gerald eagerly. And he sprang towards her with a light in his face which caused poor little Peggy's eyes to fill with angry jealous tears.

"I am afraid I have come at the wrong time, Gerald," said the visitor, in a low voice, glancing at the crowd of gaping faces. " But I must see Mr. Beresford, and at once."

" Unfortunately that is impossible," said a wiry voice from a long way below her. And the tiny housekeeper, anxious to recover her lost prestige, barred the way to the inner *salon*, to which the lady was advancing. " Mr. Beresford has already been over-excited to-day, and I cannot allow him to be disturbed."

Some watch-dog's instinct had told her that the visit of the beautiful stranger would be an unwelcome one.

" I must insist, I am afraid," said Madame de Lancry coolly ; " I have come on a matter of life and death."

She made a step further towards the door of the inner *salon*, when it was opened from the other side, and Mr. Beresford himself gently tried to push Miss M'Leod out of the way.

" Come in here, madame, if you please," said he, in a voice that was scarcely steady.

And Miss M'Leod felt, as she glanced up

at the cruel handsome mouth and steely glowing eyes of the strange lady, who seemed to sweep her out of the way as if she had been a fly, that her instinct of mistrust was a right one.

CHAPTER IX.

As soon as they were alone together in the little *salon*, Mr. Beresford laid his feeble hand on the back of a chair near the fire, and begged Madame de Lancry to take it.

" Thank you," said she, seating herself on an ottoman that was nearer to his own arm-chair, " I would rather sit where we can see each other."

" Certainly, madame."

The green shade he habitually wore over his eyes made the privilege one-sided ; but Madame de Lancry watched the little she could see of her companion's face as she went on talking.

" You will forgive my intrusion, I think, Mr. Beresford, when I tell you that I have just learned that a man in whom you are as

much interested as I am lies under suspicion
of a crime which *you* know and *I* know he
has not committed."

Mr. Beresford's perfect self-possession for a
moment left him.

" Indeed !" he said huskily, without looking at his visitor ; "your statement is very
sensational, very startling, madame."

" It is more than that. A warrant has
been issued in England for the arrest of the
man Blair, on suspicion of his being the murderer of Mr. Shaw. Now, *I* know and *you*
know that the real criminal was quite another
person "—whether this were a random shot
or not, its effect on the paralytic was sudden
and strong—" and I want you to help me,
not to bring the guilty man to justice, but to
prevent his crime from hurting the innocent."

" Really, I—I am not in a fit state of
health to bear all this exciting talk——"

" You are strong enough to hear one thing :
Mr. Shaw was murdered at the very time
when he was going to prove Blair's innocence, and to befriend Gerald Staunton
actively. On learning the death of the man

on whom he relied, Blair has not dared to
show himself, and therefore he now lies under
suspicion both of the theft and of the murder.
Gerald remains in his old position of under-
paid clerk. The wrongs of these two men
have to be righted."

"Very likely, madame, but it's not my
work."

The paralytic's manner grew cooler and
drier as the lady became more excited.

"Then it will be mine."

Mr. Beresford slowly shifted his position a
little, and leaned back as if amused.

"Most kind and womanly. If talking
would do them any good, I am sure you will
do your best for them."

"Believe me, it would be so much wiser
of you to do the work for me."

"I never guessed a riddle in my life,
madame, so if you will explain your melodramatic threats—for I suppose you are
threatening me—we shall get over the ground
more quickly."

"Very well, then. Your philanthropy in
keeping Gerald Staunton here is a sham ; you

have no personal regard, no pity for him whatever. You took him up merely to keep him off the track of his father's murderer."

Her words might have been the ravings of a madwoman for all the effect they had on the paralytic. There was a pause before he answered her.

"I'm sure his father's murderer ought to be very much obliged to me."

Madame de Lancry was not more easily disconcerted than he.

"Believe me, you will increase and not lessen his obligation to you by doing what I ask."

"You have asked nothing, madame."

"I ask you, first, to recompense Gerald Staunton for his six long years of exile and misfortune, for his clouded name, for his services to you—by giving him your daughter in marriage. I ask you to find some means—I don't care what means—to rescue the man Blair from his position as a suspected thief and murderer."

"Your demands are certainly modest. And what is to be my reward? The satis-

faction of having done two good deeds? I
am not philanthropic."

"But you are prudent. Let M. de Breteuil know what my demands are, and ask
him whether it would not be better to accede
to them."

"It is ten years since you were the mis-
tress of M. de Breteuil—you see my knowledge of your history is as extensive as and more
accurate than yours of mine—may not your
influence over him have waned since then?"

"My power over him has not. Ten years
ago I knew one desperate secret of his; now
I know two. Shall I give you the details of
both? I have no doubt you know enough
about them to be able to judge of my
accuracy."

Madame de Lancry sat upright and spoke
calmly; she might have passed for a statue
of Justice but for the steady fire that burned
in her gray eyes, which betrayed that this
was not with her a mere question of abstract
right and wrong. The paralytic moved nervously in his chair.

"For God's sake be quiet," said he, in a

low voice, watching her uneasily from under
the shade over his eyes. "What difference
can it make to you who marries my
daughter?"

"We'll say it is a whim of mine that
Gerald should marry her. Knowing my
history, as you say you do, you will not
be surprised that I have whims."

There was just a shade of increased confidence in her tone, and the paralytic noticed
this.

"And what if I refuse, madame?"

"Then I shall use my knowledge of M. de
Breteuil's secrets as I please."

"And how will that affect me?"

"By affecting those in whom you have an
interest."

"An interest! What interest?"

"Shall I tell you?"

She could only see the lower part of his
face, the curved nostrils, the drooping white
moustache, and reverend white beard; but as
she looked, trying to define the lips half
hidden by the silver hair, she drew back her
head with a slight start, and a cry, which she

tried to stifle, broke from her. Raising his left hand, Mr. Beresford slowly pushed up the green shade that was over his eyes; the light from the lamp made him blink, but he returned her gaze steadily, and watched the change which instantly took place in her look and manner. Her confidence gave way to doubt, doubt to utter confusion; after a few moments' silence her eyes fell and her head dropped.

"Won't you explain yourself, madame?" said Mr. Beresford urbanely. "You were going to be kind enough to tell me the nature of my interest in Mr. Shaw's murderer."

"I made a mistake," said Madame de Lancry, rising hurriedly. "I confess I felt convinced I recognised in you an old boulevard acquaintance of M. de Breteuil's, and your knowledge of my past history seemed to confirm that."

"An acquaintance is not necessarily an accomplice, madame."

"No, no—but—your manner seemed to me suspicious when I spoke of M. de Breteuil's—secrets."

"Every man has secrets, I among the
rest. You judge very hastily."

"And apologise very humbly. I hope you
will forget and forgive my intrusion, monsieur."

She held her hand down to him in winning,
gracious apology. The austere old man gave
way a little.

"A lady's impulsive kindness of heart will
get the better of her judgment sometimes,"
said he indulgently. "You take a very warm
interest in Gerald, madame."

He did not take her proffered hand, but
pointed to a chair. Madame de Lancry,
however, bowed, and walked towards the
door.

"I have had an adventurous youth, and I
am passing into a dull middle age : two good
reasons for my being quixotically and roman-
tically kind-hearted—by fits and starts. After
this abortive outburst, I have no doubt the
volcano will slumber peacefully for a twelve-
month, at least."

She laughed, in the most light-hearted and
charming manner, and wished him good-even-

ing, as if her errand had been about bonbons.
And Mr. Beresford chuckled civilly in return, as if any errand would have been welcome that brought him such a fascinating
guest. But the artificial grin left both faces
as soon as they were out of each other's sight;
and both grew grave and hard, as if the interview had brought each in contact with a new
enemy.

In the outer *salon* Madame de Lancry had
some difficulty in escaping from old M. Fournier, whose elaborate compliments and civili-
ties she received with the manner of a tired
empress. Victor did not come near her until
called by his father, and then he stood by
rather shyly, without looking at the beautiful
lady, all his vivacity suddenly gone. He was
quite eclipsed for the time by the quiet Gerald,
who shook Madame de Lancry's hand warmly
in both his, and begged her to sit down on
the chair he brought, and hung over her
affectionately when she had done so. The
ladies rather held aloof, as if feeling that
there must be something improper in this

beauty, this stateliness, and the devotion they excited in the less particular sex.

Madame Fournier, good soul, who came of an ugly race, and looked upon handsome people as eccentricities of Nature that should not be judged too harshly, tried to heal the breach by a well-meaning but tactless inquiry when Madame de Lancry and M. le Général would leave Calais.

" Not for some time, I think," answered Madeline suavely. " I have just made up my mind to ask my husband to take a house a little way out of the town for a few months ; the place is so cheerful and the society so charming."

Victor glanced uneasily round to see how his relations took this speech ; but it excited nothing more than surprise in most of them.

" I don't think you will find it so gay if you settle down here," said Madame Fournier doubtfully.

" And poultry is so dear here !" hazarded a cousin ; adding hurriedly, with an awkward laugh, " but of course that would not affect you, madame."

"No," said Madame de Lancry slowly, as she rose to go, "it will not affect me much, for while I am here I shall live upon—excitement."

The ladies present came one and all to the conclusion that Madame de Lancry was mad; but the gentlemen viewed her eccentricities more leniently.

"I could never have believed that I should have found a romantic, robber-haunted district so near to civilization," she went on. "I really feel a delicious dread of being attacked on my way back to Calais."

And she glanced at Gerald. Before he could offer to escort her back, however, Victor sprang forward with open jealousy burning in his face.

"Let me go with you, madame; no one knows the road so well as I do."

Madame de Lancry laughed as she laid her hand on Gerald's arm.

"What would your poor little *fiancée* say?" said she, in a low voice, which, however, Peggy's keen little ears overheard.

"Oh, you may take him, madame; I don't

mind," she broke in with alacrity, glancing alternately at Gerald and the beautiful lady with open disapproval of their friendly attitude.

" You are not jealous, then ?" said Madame de Lancry, playfully raising the unwilling little face and bending to look straight into the elfish eyes.

" Not of—Victor," answered Peggy boldly, but in so low a whisper that it needed the sidelong look of anger she cast at Gerald to make her meaning clear.

Madame de Lancry kept the indignant face between her hands for a few moments longer, her interest evidently deepening as she looked. Then she turned very suddenly, to try to get the light of the lamp upon the girl's face. But Peggy wriggled herself out of the lady's grasp, and, plunging into the group of which Madame Fournier formed a member, put her head into the motherly lap and effaced herself.

Victor, who had recovered his self-possession, wisely refrained from forming one of the party that gathered in the hall to see

Madame de Lancry off, but devoted himself to dispelling the momentary consternation caused by his behaviour to her, with animation still more marked, still less spontaneous than before. No one guessed how he loathed every member of the dull society he was entertaining, and how madly he envied—for the moment—the gentle English lad Madame de Lancry so unaccountably and openly preferred to him.

The little square omnibus which had brought the unexpected visitor to "Les Bouleaux" rumbled slowly for some distance on the road back to Calais before either of its occupants broached any subject of particular interest to them. Gerald felt shy of doing so, and Madame de Lancry was not talkative.

"So that little wild girl is the queen of women!" she said at last, smiling rather contemptuously, as he thought.

"Yes, madame," he answered, feeling hot and not very happy, but resolved to stick to his colours.

"Well, I have examined her and thought

over the situation, and I think it would be much better for you to give her up."

"I know that, madame," said he simply; "but no fellow worth the name of a man ever does give up a girl for that reason. Besides, you can't give up what you haven't got, and what you never had a chance of getting. Please don't talk about her. It won't make any difference, and I can't explain myself, and it only makes me look like a fool."

"Well, what shall we talk about, then?"

"Won't you tell me why you came to see Mr. Beresford? I can't help thinking it was about—about that awful night's work; and I know you went to see old Monnier about it. You have told me just enough to make me half mad to know more."

"What do you want to know?"

"The name of the man who killed my father. Only tell me, and I will hunt him out and——"

"That is unnecessary, for I know where he is."

Gerald started violently.

"Tell me, for God's sake, tell me!" said he hoarsely; "I would give anything for something to do now—like that."

And in the dusk she saw on the young man's face the hungry look brought by unsatisfied passion, and she knew that the tool was growing sharper for the work.

"I cannot tell you. For I have so little proof of what I have told you, that if the murderer were arrested now, he would be able to prove that on the night Mr. Shaw died he was where he is now—two hundred miles away."

Gerald's face changed.

"It is cruel of you to play with me like this, madame," said he, with bitterness and energy most unusual in him. "You led me to believe——"

"What I believed myself—that I had a clue between my very fingers. I have found out to-day that I was mistaken—that the work before us is not even begun."

"Well, how am I to begin it? Give me something to do, some reason for getting away from this place, or I think I shall go mad."

"Ah!" broke out Madame de Lancry rather bitterly. "It is the girl, always the girl, who is in your head. If you could have her and be happy with her, you would soon forget all about clearing your father's name."

"You are hard upon me, madame. I have nursed the hope of avenging him so long and so vainly that it hangs about me like an old dream, and I can hardly take in the belief that it will ever be realized."

"And the other hope—isn't that a vain one too?"

"Yes, I—I suppose so."

"Oh, then you have still some idea of entering the lists with Victor, and coming off conqueror after all!"

Gerald stared at her in wounded astonishment. She had always shown the best side of her nature to him before, so that her sneers were disconcerting.

"No, I haven't, madame," he said at last. "But if one were to let all one's hopes go out at once, one wouldn't get on very well, and—I suppose you don't know what it is to —to be quite cracked about anyone?" And he looked at her with shy admiration. " But can't you understand how the fellows felt who were cracked about you ?"

She turned towards him with a sudden gust of kindness, as if he had struck the right note at last.

"Yes, Gerald, perhaps I can," she said. " And it is true that you can do nothing until I have found out something for you to do."

" It's awfully good of you to take so much interest in this business."

" Good ! No, that is not the right word. Disinterested help is weak and capricious. Luckily for you, in helping you I am helping myself."

Gerald watched her face silently for a few moments, and then said quietly: "I think I understand. You have some grudge of your own against the man who killed my father ?"

" Yes."

" And you have been brooding over it all these years, just as I have done ?"

"No. I had almost forgotten it when chance—or—or perhaps something higher— brought me face to face with you. Then I remembered, having nothing better to do, that I had a promise to keep and an oath to fulfil: the promise concerned you, Gerald, and the oath concerned your father's murderer."

The young man said nothing. This woman's nature, that could lie calm so long, and then be stirred by strong waves of passionate impulse, was quite a new and inexplicable thing to him; and her cynical suggestion that she had set herself to this bloodhound's task for want of anything better to do excited in him alarm and mistrust. He glanced at her shyly and waited for her to explain herself.

But as the little omnibus began to rattle through the stone - paved Calais streets, Madame de Lancry shook off her melodramatic mood, and teased the poor lad by talking of nothing but trifles; and when they reached the door of the Hôtel de la Gare he helped her to alight in a rather crestfallen manner.

"Good-night, madame," said he hesitatingly, as she was sweeping past him into the hotel.

"Oh, come in," she said lightly, glancing behind her at him.

"But Mr. Beresford will not like me to stay away longer; I know it will displease him very seriously."

"Mr. Beresford's freaks need no longer disturb you. You are not going back to 'Les Bouleaux.'"

She laid her hand firmly on the arm of the astonished lad, and drew him within the doorway, speaking at the same time in a very quiet and careless voice.

"Do you know where Mr. Smith is, Gerald ?"

"Mr. Smith! He is in London."

"You know his address ?"

"Oh yes; I write him long letters at Mr. Beresford's dictation very often."

"That's all right. Now come upstairs, and we'll see what we can do to equip you for a night journey. You must cross to England to-night."

CHAPTER X.

GERALD STAUNTON heard Madame de Lancry's mandate very calmly, and let her lead him upstairs into her sitting-room unresistingly. But no sooner had she closed the door, and looked well at his face by the light of the candles, which had been burning some time in anticipation of her return, than she saw that she had overrated his docility.

"I am sorry I can't do what you wish, madame, for you have been very kind to me. But I could not think of going to England without Mr. Beresford's permission. Goodnight."

He was at the door before he finished speaking, and would have been out of the room in another moment, if Madame de Lancry had not darted across the room with the lightness of a girl, and caught both his hands in a grip so unexpectedly savage and muscular that Gerald instinctively tried to wrest himself free as angrily as if she had been a man.

" Wait !" she said, looking straight into his indignant face with lurid, dilated eyes. " What has Mr. Beresford ever done for you that you haven't overpaid him for ? What clerk in his office has worked so hard as you, or received so little pay for it ? What has he ever done to make your life worth living ? Can you doubt now that it would have been better to beg your way back to England, when he picked you up in Paris six years ago, than to spend the best years of your life in the dull drudgery from which he never means to set you free ? You want to find the man who killed your father—Mr. Beresford wants to keep you off the track. Break away from this man now—it may be your last chance. Follow my instructions, find out your old friends, and there is still time for you to clear your father's name and to live a happy life in your own country. I give you my solemn word you are not even safe in this one!"

Gerald's face grew white and wet as he looked at her, and heard the burning words she was hissing into his ear like an enchantress. At the end, he tried again to free himself from her grasp, with the manner of a man who is shrinking from some spell.

"I cannot go, madame. He is my employer at least, if he is not my benefactor."

She drew back a little way from him suddenly, without releasing him, and, as she spoke again, her voice was no longer whisperingly persuasive, but rang out in sharp clear tones like a bell.

"Do you know," she said, "that it is your presence at ' Les Bouleaux' that is hastening Miss Beresford's marriage with young Fournier ?"

The young man's limbs began to twitch and to tremble, and he was again like wax in her hands. She pressed her advantage instantly.

"The old man knows of your fancy for his daughter. He does not care a straw for any pain you may feel, and he will avoid all danger from a possible return of your affection by marrying her before your eyes, within a few days, to this man, who does not love her. Are you willing to witness this?"

"My going away would not change Mr. Beresford's plans. You do not know him," said Gerald hoarsely.

"My poor boy, you have no one else to trust. You may as well trust me," said she, with a change in tone and manner to caressing softness, as she again drew nearer to him. "If you will do as I wish, and cross to England to-night, I will not only get you Mr. Beresford's permission to remain away, but I will swear to you that his daughter shall marry no one against her own will."

Gerald raised his head, breathing heavily, and looked with dull, dazed eyes wistfully into the passionate, hard, yet swiftly-changing face before him.

"I must go—away—from her?" he said brokenly. "You will only be good to her if I do that? Madame, why don't you explain? I am not a child. It is not fair to push me blindly on in the dark. What power is it you have over us all ?"

" Simply the power of a wilful woman, my dear boy ; but there is nothing in the world like it," said Madame de Lancry, dropping some of her tragic earnestness the moment that it had made sufficient impression.

" And you want me to trust only to that ?"

" Ah, you are not yet bribed heavily enough !" she broke out impatiently. " It is not enough for you that the girl should be safe : she must be safe with you. Well, then, follow my instructions for the next week, and you shall be free to marry the girl—if you will."

The magnetic influence of this woman's glowing beauty, and passionate, capricious earnestness, was so strong that a tide of joy rushed up in the young man's heart, and swept away all doubt as to her power of fulfilling her promises.

" I—I will go, madame," he said, almost staggering, as at last he felt himself free from her strong grasp.

And he turned towards the door, his brain

dizzy, his senses quickened, his heart on fire. A faint sigh of relief, which involuntarily escaped from the lady's lips, roused his dulled conscience, however, and he turned, not irresolute, but with resolution changed.

" I will go to ' Les Bouleaux,' and ask Mr. Beresford to let me return to England; if, as you say, he wants to get rid of me, no doubt he will let me go at once, and I will come and receive your orders."

" You are under my orders now," said she imperiously, turning him like a child from the door, and half forcing him into a chair beside the stove. " You will not leave this hotel except to go straight to the boat, and by the time you arrive in London you will find Mr. Beresford's permission to remain there awaiting you."

Gerald did not try to resist any longer. He sat as if stupefied, answering with an effort the remarks his hostess made on indifferent subjects as she opened her writing-case and prepared to write letters. As he furtively watched her movements, Gerald was surprised to see that her manner of setting herself to this task was fussily feminine—not at all simple and business-like, as he would have expected from her strength of will and firmness of purpose. In the midst of her busy play with blotting-paper and penwiper, the door opened, and a gentleman, whom Gerald guessed to be M. de Lancry, came in. He glanced from Gerald, who rose, to his wife, who nodded to him, and saying briefly, " Mr. Staunton, a young friend of mine," went on with her occupation.

So the old and young man sat meekly down, and, after the exchange of a few commonplaces, the two seemed to take to each other, and, as the lady left them entirely to themselves, they chatted very amicably for some time, until the General, who persisted in speaking laborious English in spite of Gerald's efforts to keep him on more familiar ground, asked him what Madame de Lancry was doing for him.

" Some trouble with your sweetheart, and my wife make it up ?" he suggested good-humouredly.

" No," said Gerald, growing suddenly shy

and husky, "I haven't a sweetheart, monsieur."

"Oh, tell me not that ; no, no," said the General, laughing ; " if not a sweetheart for ever, still, a sweetheart for to-day."

"No, monsieur," said the young fellow, who was scarlet by this time ; "a sweetheart for ever is not so easy to get, and a sweetheart for to-day would not satisfy me."

"Right, very right," said the General, nodding his head slowly from time to time to eke out his laboured sentences. " Give up love for pleasure when you are young, and when you are old you get neglect in the stead of either."

Involuntarily Gerald's eyes stole, after this gloomy speech, from the grave old soldier to his still young and handsome wife. She rose abruptly from the table, and rang the bell, saying that Gerald must have supper before his journey.

" You travel to-night ?" asked the General, surprised.

" Yes, monsieur ; I am going to London."

" Ah, there, among your beautiful countrywomen, you will find the sweetheart for ever."

"No, monsieur," confessed Gerald simply; "I am leaving her behind."

And the old and the young man exchanged looks of quiet sympathy as their *tête-à-tête* broke up.

From that moment—perhaps guessing the danger that the young man's firmness might fail him if he were allowed time for reflection about this separation from the girl he loved— Madame de Lancry never left him one moment to himself or to her husband; and, when the time drew near for the departure of the boat, she sent for her mantle, and herself accompanied him to the quay, leaning on his arm, and enchaining his unwilling and wandering attention by kind questions about himself, his tastes, his pleasures, and his prospects. She was so sweet, so sympathetic, that he blamed himself for not feeling more grateful, and, as he shook her hand before stepping on board, he said humbly:

"You must think me a great bear, Madame de Lancry, for not saying more to you about what you have done, and have promised to do. But——"

" Thanks given for promises are always unsubstantial things," she interrupted, laughing. " In a month from now you shall fall at my feet and bless me."

Then she shook both his hands again heartily, and watched him as he made his way amongst the crowd of passengers hurrying on board the boat. She had intentionally waited for the arrival of the Paris train before bringing him down to the quay, and even now she followed him carefully with her eyes as he walked about the boat in search of a seat. When the gangway was drawn up she breathed more freely ; but it was not until the boat had steamed away, and Gerald raised his hat to her, with a safe distance of some fifty yards between him and the shore, that her face relaxed and lost its expression of eager anxiety. Then she walked briskly to the end of the pier, and looked out over the dark shifting sea at the boat as it became a speck in the distance. Then she laughed, neither musically nor sweetly, and turned back towards the hotel.

"Poor boy," she said to herself, with real pity in her voice, "it is not quite fair, perhaps, to trick him ; and he is not the sort of man I should have chosen for his task, if I had been able to choose. But one must use such tools as come to one's hand, and he will do as well as another if he will only follow my instructions."

These instructions, so far, had been very simple. Gerald had only to go to Mr. Smith's London lodgings, to put a letter from Madame de Lancry into his hands, and then to remain in London until he heard from her again.

On the following morning Madame de Lancry drove to "Les Bouleaux," and arrived there just as Mr. Beresford came downstairs. In spite of Miss M'Leod's entreaties, he insisted on receiving the visitor himself.

"I won't trouble you long, Mr. Beresford," said his tormentor sweetly, as she was ushered into his presence, and advanced towards him with a hand most sympathetically outstretched.

He gravely raised her fingers to his lips with his left hand, and thanked her for her kindness in visiting a tiresome old invalid so often.

"Not at all," said she imperturbably. "We had such a pleasant interview yesterday that it is a pleasure to come again."

"You have come to tell me that you have brought my boy Gerald safely back, I hope, madame. I should have been nervous about him last night, if he had not been in such good hands."

"It is very kind of you to say so. He is now in good hands, better even than mine; for I have sent him back to his friends in England. Ah, I knew you would be grateful," she broke out suddenly, in a different tone, as Mr. Beresford gave a slight but perceptible start. "There is no doubt he would have proved a serious obstacle to your daughter's marriage—girls are quick to find out who loves them best—and you have borne the generous burden of the boy's maintenance too long."

" You have taken a most———"

" Unwarrantable liberty ? Yes, I have. But you will forgive me, won't you ? And now that the boy is once away, you will write him permission to stay away, will you not ? He is at the Charing Cross-Hotel. See how perfectly frank I am with you : I have given you his address, so that you can recall him if you like; but still—I would advise you to let him remain in England."

The autocrat was cowed. He took up a pencil in his trembling left hand, and played with it and with a sheet of paper nervously.

" And what if I recall him ?" he said at last, very quietly.

" Then, as I have taken a fancy into my head to befriend the lad, I must do it in some other manner."

He raised his head, and his eyes, from under the green shade, peered at her once penetratingly. Then he scrawled a few lines slowly with the pencil on the sheet of paper, which he handed to her. She read it aloud :

" DEAR GERALD,

" If you want a holiday, you are welcome to it. Let me hear from you.

" Yours affectionately,

" MARTIN BERESFORD."

" Very kind of you," murmured Madame de Lancry softly. " May I send this to the boy ?"

" If you please, madame," said the paralytic indifferently.

And with profuse apologies for disturbing him so early, Madame de Lancry left him. In the hall she met the autocrat's little dragon guardian, to whom she bowed most graciously.

" How is Miss Beresford, after the excitement of yesterday ? These betrothal dinners are trying ordeals."

" I cannot inform you, madame," said the housekeeper stiffly. " Miss Beresford ran out of the house this morning before breakfast, in a fit of petulance, and has not returned."

And, with a sweeping curtsey, Miss M'Leod
retreated into the *salon* without another
word.

On re-entering the hired carriage in which
she had come, Madame de Lancry gave the
direction—" Fabrique Fournier, Saint Pierre."
As she drove along the straight sandy road
she saw, a little before the point where the
canal comes in sight, the small, slight figure
of a shabbily-dressed girl hurrying along at
the side of the road. Madame de Lancry
glanced at her carelessly, but did not recog-
nise her as anyone she had seen before.
On arriving at the factory, she sent in a
message, asking whether M. Victor Fournier
could spare her a few minutes. She had
scarcely time to lean back in the carriage
when the young fellow hurried out to her,
flushed and radiant at the unexpected sight of
her.

" Are you very busy ?" said she, smiling
with her most persuasive manner.

" I am never too busy to be at your
commands, madame."

" Then come with me a little way. I'm

so dull; I haven't seen anybody but my husband since—yesterday."

The impressionable young Frenchman opened the carriage-door promptly, and took the seat she offered him beside her.

"Where shall I tell him to drive to, madame?"

"Oh, anywhere, anywhere—out of the town for a little while."

More pleased than ever, Victor told the coachman to take the Guînes road, and then turned to the lady, still scarcely believing in his own good fortune. Among the local pseudo-beauties he was considered dangerous by his rivals, irresistible by himself; but this fascinating new-comer belonged to another world, and with her one could not be so sure of one's powers.

How charming she was, he thought, as she leant back, without taking the pains to be extremely vivacious, as one half of the ladies he knew capable of this sort of adventure would have been, or inconceivably languid, like the remaining half! How sweet, how new, her attitude of business-like seriousness was! It

was, in fact, so business-like, so serious, that
a moment's doubt clouded the young Frenchman's infatuated happiness.   This doubt was
deliciously dispelled by her first words.

" I am afraid I made a very inopportune
appearance at ' Les Bouleaux ' yesterday.
Your *fiancée* did not seem pleased to see
me."

" Madame, she did not know how much
reason she had to be displeased."

Madame de Lancry looked at him steadily,
but without showing either gratification or
annoyance at his words.

" You don't care for Miss Beresford,
Victor ?" she said at last.

He shrugged his shoulders.

" Madame, I care for her as one cares for
the case and the straw in which one receives
a present of choice wine : the wine could not
come without them, but when it has come,
they are in the way."

" Ah, ' les beaux yeux de sa cassette ' are
the attraction.   Why, Victor, you are avaricious at three—four-and-twenty !   What do
you want with this unfledged little creature's

dot, you who have just had a fortune left you ?"

" Ah, but, madame——" began the young man eagerly ; and then he hesitated.

" Well !"

" With that fortune there is a condition—I must marry an English girl."

Madame de Lancry started, but for a few moments she said nothing. Then she looked at him penetratingly.

" That is very strange, is it not ? You have an aunt who has not seen you since you were a child, who never cared much about you, who scarcely remembers your existence. Mr. Beresford lives in the same town with her for a few weeks ; he is avaricious, he has a marriageable daughter who has not previously occupied much of his thoughts. He returns from Nice, sends for his daughter, engages her to you, and shortly afterwards you learn that a fortune has been left you by your aunt, on condition of your marrying an English girl. Has the matter struck you in this light ?"

" Yes and no, madame. Mr. Beresford is

an oracle with my father, who sees in all this
a smart stroke of business, which he admires.
They are partners, and what is good for
one is good for both. I almost think that,
on condition of this arrangement, my father
has consented to my receiving with Miss Beresford no *dot* at all."

"Does not that seem strange? Your
father is a rich man ; so must Mr. Beresford
be. Take my advice, do not let yourself be
hurried into this marriage until your aunt's
will is proved." She saw immediately that
these words were taken by the young fellow
for a flattering sign of jealousy. She added :
"What if Mr. Beresford, careful as he seems,
is imperilling his own fortune by private
speculation ? That is what the erratic
conduct of his confidential clerk Smith
suggests to me."

Victor, who was in debt, took the alarm at
once.

"What can I do, madame ? I dare not
hint such a thing to my father. I cannot
prove it for myself."

" Take my advice. Be on the watch for

Smith's comings and goings.   Mr. Beresford
is in feeble health : you are deeply in love, of
course, with his daughter.   Make one or the
other of these excuses for constant attendance
at 'Les Bouleaux,' and watch the effect of
Mr. Smith's visits on Mr. Beresford.   Speculation is gambling : watch for the gambler's
elation, the gambler's depression, the gambler's
irritability in Mr. Beresford's manner ; and if
you find the signs hard to read, come to me."

"Madame, how can I thank you ?"

" There is no need for thanks at all," said
she, with simple magnanimity, in which
Victor could detect no venom.   "I shall be
too happy if I can help you against the fraud
of a speculator or the avarice of a miser."

She told Victor to direct the driver to return ; and the young man's cupidity had been
so successfully aroused that she found no
difficulty in keeping his admiration under the
strictest control until he left the carriage at
the outskirts of the town.   She looked after
him with a shrewd expression on her face.

" A very good ferret for the second hole,"
she said to herself ; " and now for the third."

She was thoughtful and preoccupied as she drove back to the hotel, and went upstairs to her sitting-room. At the door her attention was suddenly aroused by the sound of a high, excited girl's voice inside. She turned the handle and went in, guessing who the intruder was. Her husband was sitting, silent and solemn, by the stove, and in front of him, pouring forth torrents of indignant eloquence, in the attitude of a miniature Cassandra, was Peggy Beresford.

CHAPTER XI.

THE entrance of Madame de Lancry did not in the least disconcert Peggy Beresford, who turned towards her fiercely, as if rather glad to find an opponent more worthy of her steel than the peaceful old General.

"Where is Gerald? What have you done with him?" she began at once, as Madame de Lancry walked into the room, very composedly unfastened the clasp of her fur cloak, and seated herself in a chair facing her husband's, as if the excited little intruder had been some over-indulged domestic pet whose capricious humours were of no consequence. At these fierce questions she looked up lazily.

"My good child, don't you know that these uncivilized attacks are the luxury of the very poor, and are quite out of place between

31—2

people like you and me ? Now run away home, like the good little savage you are at heart, and I will make no complaint to your father about your impertinent intrusion."

" It won't make any difference to me if you do, for I shall never see my father again if I can help it. And I won't leave this place till I know what has become of Gerald."

" Then we shall enjoy the pleasure of your society for some time, my child. Gerald Staunton is now occupied with business far too important for him to be distracted by any wild and childish whims of yours."

" Then you won't tell me where he is ?" The little creature turned, white and shaking with passionate excitement, from the hand-some lady whose face was now as hard as a mask, to her quiet old husband, who sat watching the conflict in much anxiety. " Make her tell me—do make her tell me ! You said you would help me if you could. Why don't you make her speak ?"

" Don't worry my husband, dear child. I have no doubt he would do anything in his power to assist you, but this, unfortunately, is out of his power."

She rose from her chair and opened the door with a majesty not to be resisted.

"Now go," she said, in a voice harder and colder than ever. "You have intruded upon us long enough."

Shivering from head to foot with rage, disappointment, and physical fatigue, Peggy still stood before her, and hurled forth her last defiance in tones alternately harsh and broken.

"You are a hard, selfish, cruel woman, and you have no more friendship for Gerald than you have love for your husband," she burst out tremulously. "But I will save him from you. I don't know where he is, and I haven't a penny in the world. But I will find him out, and go to him, and tell him how wicked you are, and how much I love him, if I have to beg my way all over France, and England too."

And with a smothered sob she gave up all attempt at maintaining her dignity, and rushed past her enemy out of the room.

Madame de Lancry shut the door after her
with an exclamation of relief, and turned to
ask her husband if she should read to him, as
if glad to be rid of a distasteful subject.
The General thanked her with his usual
elaborate courtesy, but he was not quite at
ease ; and she had scarcely read half a dozen
lines of an article in the *Gaulois* on the political crisis, when he turned abruptly in his
chair and interrupted her.

" Madeline, you are too good to me, as you
always are. But I will not trouble you to
read to me longer, for I cannot listen to-day.
That poor child's entreaties fill my ears.
Why were you so harsh to her, Madeline ?
You who are so gentle, so kind !"

Madame de Lancry dashed down the paper
and went to the window without answering.
The crust of her habitual calmness was
broken up, and passion was flashing in her
great eyes. The General rose slowly from
his chair, followed her to the window, and
called her softly, " Madeline, Madeline."

She shook her shoulder petulantly, but did
not turn.

"Madeline, you will answer me, I am sure. You are never discourteous to me."

There was such simple dignity in his appeal that she reluctantly moved so that he could see her side-face, and bent her head slightly to show that she was listening.

"Tell me what made you so unlike yourself to that poor little girl. Why were you so unkind to her? You spoke to her as if you hated her."

She turned suddenly and met him face to face. Leaning against the window-frame, with the sinking April sun shining on her chestnut hair, and on her glittering, feverish eyes, she showed her husband, for the first time in their married life, what manner of woman it was that he had married. Like the Circe of fable, like the Messalina of history, like the fairest, most daring incarnation of all that is beautiful and evil, she stood before him with the fierce lightning of reckless passion playing over her beautiful face.

"I do hate her!" She hissed the words out defiantly, and met his astonished gaze

with eyes still on fire. "And I am not
unlike myself; I am myself again."

"I don't understand you, Madeline.
What has changed you like this ?"

"I am not changed. You don't change a
letter by tearing off the envelope. The
envelope has been torn off to-day for the first
time ; if you don't like the contents of the
letter, why, you can throw it away."

She tossed back her hair with one hand
from her burning forehead, and made a step
away from the window towards the door.
Her husband touched the fingers of her right
hand reverently to detain her.

"Don't leave me like that, Madeline ; I
have not treated you so badly as to deserve
that. You do not care for me, I know ; but
you have borne with me, and I have
worshipped you even for that. No change in
you can make me love you less ; give me
your confidence, for the sake of an old
husband's love."

Madeline stopped and stared at him, hearing in her husband's tones a strange echo of
the passion which had thrilled her own voice

in the long past days when she had been a slave to the cold and selfish Louis de Breteuil. She tried to laugh, but broke off suddenly.

"I — I am behaving very foolishly, monsieur," she said, not quite steadily, making a strong effort to recover her usual indifferent manner. "If you will allow me to go to my room for a quarter of an hour, I will undertake not to trouble you with any more eruptions."

"No, no, Madeline," said the . General, seizing her hand, "you shall stay with me; you shall answer my questions now. If I let you go, you will come back in ten minutes cold, calm, listless, obedient, and I shall see no more of my wife than I see every day. Great heavens, Madeline, I am not so old nor so cold as you think, and I like you better as a devil than as a statue!"

He bent his still handsome head till his iron-gray moustache touched his wife's chestnut hair, and she submitted to be led back by him to the chair she had so abruptly left.

"Now tell me what you please," said he, seating himself beside her.

Madeline had been so long used to treating her husband as a cipher that it was for the first few moments rather disconcerting for her to be called upon to treat him as a man. As he waited quite patiently for her confidence, however, she at last rather hesitatingly gave it.

"I have met lately, quite by chance, a person—some people—who caused me great unhappiness when I was a girl, long before I ever met you."

"But this child, this little creature who was here to-day! Surely she——" Madeline's face grew sullen again.

"No, I never saw her until yesterday."

"And your reason for hating her?"

"That I cannot tell you. At least," she added quickly, "the girl is in my way. She is in love with a lad in whom I take an interest, and who would be better without her. That is reason enough, isn't it?"

And Madeline got up, with a very evident intention of answering no more questions. Her husband let her go, but he was not at all satisfied with her last explanation. If his wife had been fond of him, it would never have occurred to him to be jealous of a lad like Gerald. But, stirred as he had been by her excitement, awakened suddenly to consciousness of the strong current which ran under the crust of her everyday manner, he was ready to accept the unlikely, and he walked up and down the room, when his wife had left him, with almost a young man's impetuosity.

"A boy like that! It is impossible that she can care for him!" he said to himself, forgetting his invalid's gait as he stamped angrily upon the floor. "Why, he doesn't even care for her; it's this little girl he is thinking about. And yet, what is this business of hers that he is so busy with? And what does she mean by having these secrets from me? I won't allow it, I won't allow it! She surrounds me with an army of doctors and servants, and doses me, and walks on tiptoe near me, in order that I may treat her as a nurse and not as a wife. But I'll send them all away; I'll have no more pillows and no more walking-sticks;

I'll enter the lists myself with these young popinjays whom she doesn't even think it necessary to introduce me to. I've been deceived in her; I'll let her see she has been deceived in me."

And the General walked up to the window against which she had leaned, and pictured her again to himself as she had stood there in her proud beauty; and forgotten fire came into his own eyes as he did so. He was on the point of turning away, to give effect straightway to some of his new resolutions, when, as he glanced out upon the quay, the small figure of the girl whose appearance had raised the day's storm caught his eye. She was standing with her back towards him, looking at a ship which was being loaded for departure. A gendarme watched her idly from a few yards off, and a couple of tiny *gamins* played hide-and-seek round her, without her appearing conscious of their presence. The General was interested; she looked so forlorn, so friendless; he wondered what was the thought in her mind that kept her there alone, motionless, minute after minute. For

more than half an hour she remained in the
same place, never once moving sufficiently
for him to see her face as he sat watching
her. At last a group began to gather, the
last preparations were being made, the ship
was going to start. Peggy slunk out of the
way of the little crowd, and wandered along
under the hotel windows, glancing behind her
now and then wistfully at the busy sailors she
had been watching; and so, slowly, forlornly,
walking with wavering, uncertain steps, as if
she had no particular object in her lonely
ramble, she passed out of the General's sight
along the broad stones of the quay. He was
not satisfied; he got up and fetched his field-
glass—a toy which his wife took care to have
always at hand, as it kept him quiet—and
after allowing sufficient time for a person to
cross the movable bridge at the end of the
quay, and to get round to the opposite side of
the basin, he began to look out carefully.
Before he had watched many minutes he saw
again the tiny figure, a mere speck in the
distance by this time, moving along more
slowly than ever, stopping from time to time

to look down into the green water many feet below her. A shudder passed over the General, and a fear lest the thoughts in the poor child's mind should be darker than he had imagined : when she passed again out of sight behind the hill, he watched, in anxiety which absorbed his own troubles, for her return within range of his glass. The sky was darkening towards evening when, to his great relief, he saw the solitary speck return-ing : the warmth of the April day was gone by this time; he shut the window and shivered. His wife had not come back to renew her usual perfunctory attentions, and he was glad of it. Ringing the bell, he ordered his servant to bring him his over-coat and cap, and when the astonished man obeyed, he put them on and looked at himself in the glass with some simple satisfaction. The long military cloak which he still affected suited him, and his wife had that afternoon awakened his innocent vanity.

" You are not going out, monsieur, and so late !" remonstrated the servant, in amaze-ment. " What will madame say ?"

His master drew himself up.

"The ladies are too nervous, Charles; one should not always consult them."

And he took the strong stick he habitually used, and, refusing any other support, made his way slowly along the corridor and down the stairs. He was not strong yet, but he was in better health than he had been allowed to imagine, and he found the evening breeze that blew in his face as he stepped upon the quay rather refreshing than chilling. He turned to the left, keeping close to the water-side, and kept a sharp look-out for the little figure of which he was in search. The masts of the ships that lined the harbour were standing out black against the deepening crimson of the evening sky when he came at last face to face with Peggy Beresford.

She did not know him, but came straight towards him with a blank, sightless look on her face that made her more like an elf than ever. He stopped short in front of her, but, without even glancing up to see who it was that was barring her passage, she stepped nimbly on one side and passed him. He turned round and called to her.

"Mademoiselle!" he began, without any effect.

The sound of his limping footsteps as he hobbled after her, however, arrested her attention, and as he came up with her she turned.

"Monsieur de Lancry?" said she shyly, uncertainly, and as if prepared for flight.

"Yes, mademoiselle. Do not be alarmed. I wish to help you if you will allow me. You wish to know where is' M. Gérald."

Peggy started.

"You said you couldn't tell me!" said she sharply.

"I cannot tell you with exactness, mademoiselle ; but I know that he is in London."

"Ah, I thought so. And Madame de Lancry sent him there !"

"You are anxious to find him, mademoiselle ?" said the General stiffly.

"I *will* find him," answered Peggy, with fire, "if I have to go crying his name all through London, like the Saracen lady did Gilbert à Becket's!"

"And when do you propose to start, mademoiselle?"

All her valour went out suddenly, and she stood before him, limp and wretched, with the tears forcing their way to her eyes.

"I'll ask the captain of the night-boat to take me over," said she tremulously. "And if he won't, I'll ask the captain of the boat that goes to-morrow!"

"But he will perhaps know you. I believe you are the daughter of a gentleman who resides here."

"I don't care," muttered Peggy, whom objections made dogged; "I'll get to London somehow, if I have to sw-w-im."

"I—er—I hope—I trust that mademoiselle will not think I wish to be impertinent —I have indeed no such intention—but if I might presume to lend mademoiselle the amount necessary——"

He need not have been afraid. Peggy had scarcely got an inkling of his meaning when she made a frantic effort to embrace him on the open quay ; and clinging to his arm, with the tears running down her cheeks, she blessed him and thanked him vaguely but affectionately, while he took out his pocket-book and put five sovereigns into her hand.

" English money will be the most useful," he explained, as he put it carefully into her shaking little fingers.

" I shan't want it all," said Peggy, " I dare say."

" Too much is better than too little," said the General. " When will you start ?"

" To-night, of course."

" And what will you do with yourself in the mean time ?"

" Go to Gerald's pastrycook's and have some tarts."

" You ought to have something more solid."

" No, no, I'm all right, monsieur ; I could live upon air now."

And the tiny creature raised her weird eyes to his, and showed him a face trans-figured into loveliness by the change from anxiety and despair to energy and hope.

" Good-bye, good-bye, monsieur.　You

have been a fairy godmother to me, and I will love you all my life for it."

She seized one of his hands and printed two or three quick, passionate kisses on it; then, like a spirit of the evening mist, she fled away so quickly that, before he could even return her farewell, she was out of his sight.

The General walked very slowly the short distance which lay between him and the hotel. His wife, who had heard of his caprice, met him in consternation. But he laughed off her fears with a new indifference to his ailments, and she began to understand that the relations between herself and him were changed since the afternoon. He gave no explanation of his expedition, no reason for the fancy he had to sit up until the midnight boat had left the harbour for England.

Then he went off to bed, still reticent, but satisfied, for he knew that the poor little lady whom he had helped that evening was safe on her way to the young lover in whom his own wife took such an unaccountable and undesirable interest.

" She will find him out," he thought to himself composedly, " and he will marry her and have no time to attend to other women's affairs."

And in happy ignorance of the havoc he was doing his best to work in his wife's well-laid plans, Monsieur le Général went to sleep.

Madeline sat up later, thinking over the events of the day, and congratulating herself upon the work she had done. She had had too adventurous a life not to be superstitious; and when she had summed up the results of her labours, she shook her head and sighed doubtfully.

" It has all gone too smoothly," she said to herself. " Gerald rescued from ' Les Bouleaux ' and saved from that girl. One ferret at ' Les Bouleaux '; the second in London; Paris the only hole that remains to be watched. My husband is well enough to go away; to-morrow I find out that I am tired of Calais, and must return to the boulevards; then it is only a waiting game. And yet—and yet—I wish it had not all been arranged so easily, so simply. There's always a little ripple upon the open sea; but in the smooth water close in shore one looks out for —rocks."

END OF VOL. II.

BILLING AND SONS, PRINTERS, GUILDFORD.